She opened the kitchen door and skidded to a dead stop. She was staring directly into the muzzle of a gun.

Paralyzed, Tracy could barely draw a breath. The gun was the size of a cannon. She was ready to meet God, but she would prefer to wait until another time. Her eyesight grew blurry as her legs turned to rubber.

And then the rumble of a deep voice penetrated the fog. "Hold it right there."

She dragged her gaze away from the gun and looked up. She made out the menacing figure of a man in a dark windbreaker and jeans. The room began to spin in dizzying circles. She was going to faint. She clutched at the doorjamb to keep the world from tipping over.

Through the haze, she saw him jam the pistol into its holster. Her knees crumbled, but he caught her before she hit the floor. As though she were a child, he swept her up in his arms. Barely conscious, she tried not to cling to his neck as he carried her back to the living room. Crushed against his broad chest, she was much too aware of the power in those wide shoulders. The muscular arms that gently eased her down onto the sofa could break her into little pieces.

She kept her eyes tightly closed, but sensed him looming over her. Was he trying to decide if he should put her out of her misery? And then she heard heavy footsteps as he strode out of the room.

Too weak and shaky to move, she clenched her fists as the footsteps returned. Suddenly she felt the coolness of a damp cloth across her forehead. The wave of dizziness be~~gan to recede~~.

Clutching at ~~~~ f her courage, she open ~~~~ was holding a small le ~~~~ e - a badge attached to ~~~~ it the words "Leif Ericson

D1264178

More than Great Riches

by

Jan Washburn

For Juan + Meg –
Two of my most
favorite people.
Love,
Jan Washburn

More than Great Riches

Contact Information: info@thewildrosepress.com

Cover Art by *Nicola Martinez*

The Wild Rose Press
PO Box 708
Adams Basin, NY 14410-0706
Visit us at www.thewildrosepress.com

Publishing History
First White Rose Edition, 2009
Print ISBN: 1-60154-567-3

Published in the United States of America

Dedication

In memory of my dear Jack
With love to Linda and Heather and
their beautiful families

Acknowledgments

Many thanks to Judge Bob Prince for his legal advice and for his extensive knowledge of Plymouth County; to John Palsgrove, an authority on cars and blown rods; to Betty Lou Fogt, the handbell guru, for her red and blue circles; to Ed Martin for saving my disc and my sanity; and to Renata and Roxie Kammerer for their tips on parking in the Big Apple. Any errors are my own.

A good name is more desirable than great riches; to be esteemed is better than silver or gold.

CHAPTER I

The walls of the interrogation room were dingy beige. The glare of fluorescent bulbs highlighted the crude graffiti etched into the laminated table top. The room smelled of stale pizza, sweat, and fear. Tracy's heart pounded against her ribs like a convict beating on the bars of his cell.

"Now, Miss Dixon, let's go over it again—from the beginning." The swarthy detective tilted his chair back and eyed her with a penetrating stare. His NYPD badge identified him as "C. Diaz." The grizzled hair marked him as a hardened veteran who had heard and seen it all. He would show no mercy. "How long have you known Rick Timmons?" That gravelly voice scraped against Tracy's raw nerves.

Her palms were damp, and her mouth was dry. Her fingers still showed the smudges of fingerprint ink. She didn't know whether to be angry or frightened. The detective was convinced that she had been involved in the theft of the jewelry. Was he going to arrest her as Rick's accomplice?

"I barely know him," she whispered. "I ran into him in the lobby of my apartment house about a month ago. He was looking for a rental, but there was nothing open."

"And you never dated?"

"No. Never. Some of us eat out together occasionally at the corner diner. If Rick came in while we were there, he would join us at the table. It wasn't anything like a date."

"So, Rick Timmons isn't your boyfriend?"

Tracy paused to moisten her lips. Would she incriminate herself if she admitted that Rick singled her out, and she had been flattered by his attention? They had a lot in common. While he auditioned for a part in an off-Broadway production, she was getting up the nerve to answer a cattle call for a place in the chorus of "Aida." Over a glass of cranberry juice they discovered they were both from Massachusetts— cranberry country—Rick from Cape Cod and Tracy from Allerton in Plymouth County. At the moment, men were not her favorite species of humanity, but any woman who had a pulse would be drawn to Rick's movie star looks and charm.

The detective was growing impatient. "Miss Dixon, I asked if Rick Timmons was your boyfriend."

"No," Tracy managed. "Just an acquaintance."

"But he invited you to Ronda Starr's reception."

"No," Tracy put in quickly. "It wasn't like that. One day at the diner my roommate mentioned that I had an invitation to Miss Starr's reception. Rick said that he was invited too. He suggested that we share the cost of a cab, instead of taking the subway."

"Then you know where Timmons lives?"

"No, I don't. We agreed it would be simpler if we took the cab together from my place. I'm sure he lives nearby."

"And just how did two unknown, unemployed actors manage to wangle an invitation to the home of the biggest name on Broadway?"

"I'm not unemployed," Tracy protested. "I'm an assistant at Alan Rifkin's talent agency. I've worked there for almost three years."

The detective gave her a humorless smile. "So,

how did an agent's insignificant assistant wangle an invitation to Ronda Starr's reception?"

Tracy smothered a groan. On Sunday morning she should be in church, not in the grim confines of a police station. She could almost hear her mother's fretful voice, "What will people say?" And she had been in this grimy little room for hours. She had given Detective Diaz a complete description of Rick. She had volunteered to be fingerprinted to prove she had not touched Ronda Starr's safe. They had been over all these questions several times. She felt as though she were reciting lines in a long-running play.

She suspected Diaz made her repeat her story to catch her in a contradiction. He hoped she would accidentally reveal some new information, but there was nothing more to tell him.

She gritted her teeth and plodded on. "One evening I found a little Yorkshire terrier whimpering in front of our building. She was wearing an expensive-looking collar. When I picked her up, I found the owner's phone number on the tag, so I called."

Tracy had been flabbergasted to find that the dog's owner was Ronda Starr. "Miss Starr told me Bitsy jumped out of her car when they stopped at a traffic light. She wanted to give me a reward, but I told her I couldn't accept money just for making a simple phone call. She insisted that she would find some way to show her appreciation. When she sent her chauffeur to pick up the dog, he handed me an invitation to her reception."

"And how did your friend, Mr. Timmons, rate an invite?"

Tracy had asked herself the same question. "I don't know. He talked as though they were old friends. Maybe he acted in one of her shows." Rick had never explained his connection to Ronda Starr.

How could I have been so naïve? I should have

trusted my instincts about Rick. There was something phony about all that charm.

"Did Timmons show an invitation to the butler?"

Tracy closed her eyes, trying to recall the sequence of events. She had been so starry-eyed and excited when they climbed the steps to Miss Starr's fashionable brownstone. The whole evening played out like a dream sequence in a Broadway show.

She remembered that Rick took her arm as the butler opened the door. She thrust her precious invitation into the butler's hands, and they strolled into the elegant foyer, trying to look sophisticated and blasé. Did Rick present his own invitation or did the butler assume they were a couple?

She opened her eyes. "I don't remember," she admitted wearily. She drew a long breath and shifted her weight, trying to find a comfortable position. The stiff plastic chair was harder than the old wooden pews in the Allerton Community Church.

"Tell me about the party." The detective sounded bored, but those cynical eyes never relented.

"It was very nice." Tracy paused. *Very nice? What a totally inadequate statement. It was beyond fabulous.* A five-piece combo belted out a medley of show tunes while she gaped at the luxurious furnishings, the exotic guests, and the incredible buffet table.

"Miss Starr took me around and introduced me to everyone as the girl who found her Bitsy." Remembering, Tracy almost smiled. Ronda Starr was exactly like her stage persona—hearty and exuberant, with a voice that rattled the crystal chandeliers. And there, at her side, stood Tracy Dixon, Little Miss Nobody, shaking hands with every headliner in the city. She hoped that her jaw wasn't hanging open and that her little black dress didn't scream "small-town."

"And where was Mr. Timmons while you were meeting the elite?"

Once again Tracy closed her eyes, trying to recreate the scene. She had no recollection of seeing Rick again from the moment Ronda Starr came up to greet them. He could have been anywhere.

"I - I guess he was mixing with the crowd."

"Did Miss Starr seem to know him?"

Tracy shook her head in bewilderment. "I'm not sure. She hugged him, but she hugs everybody. She may have thought I invited him. I guess it was right after that, he just disappeared."

"So you didn't see him again that night?"

"No." Tracy was so star-struck, she wouldn't have noticed if Rick had jetted out of the room on a magic carpet.

"He didn't tell you when he decided to leave?"

"No. When the guests began to drift away, I looked for him everywhere. Nobody remembered seeing him."

"So you went home alone?"

Tracy heaved a sigh. "I went home alone."

At long last Diaz stood up, stretching his arms as though he had done a hard day's work. "All right, Miss Dixon. You're free to go. But don't leave town. We'll be talking to you again. That missing jewelry is worth at least a half million dollars. And if the butler doesn't make it, we're not talking assault and battery with a deadly weapon, we're talking murder."

****

Tracy crumpled the morning newspaper into a ball and let it drop to the floor. Pushing her stuffed panda out of harm's way, she fell back across her bed. By now, everyone in New York City had seen the banner headline, "Broadway's Ronda Starr Victim of Jewel Theft." Under the headline was a blown-up picture of Miss Starr with a dazzled Tracy clinging to her arm. The caption under the picture explained that the police questioned aspiring actress Tracy Dixon as an alleged accomplice to the crime.

Tracy groaned. She was not enjoying her fifteen minutes of fame. Saturday night at Miss Starr's was the high point of her life. Sunday at the police station should have been the low point. But today, Monday, fell below rock bottom.

When she reported to work, the office manager had thrust a letter into her hand and ordered her to leave the premises. Tracy groped to find the envelope on her nightstand, a letter from Mr. Rifkin, handwritten in his odd black scratches.

"Dear Miss Dixon,

Although your work with the Rifkin Agency has been most satisfactory, I regret that I must terminate your employment. Enclosed is my check for two weeks severance pay. While I find it hard to believe that you were involved in the theft of Miss Starr's jewelry and the injuries to her butler, I cannot afford to offend my clients. I must consider the good name of the agency.

I would advise you not to appear at the audition for 'Aida' next week. Your presence would only cause embarrassment and ill feeling for all concerned.

Yours truly, Alan Rifkin"

The good name of the agency, she thought dully. *Does anyone care about the good name of Tracy Dixon?*

She felt like the little man in the comic strips who lived under a thundercloud that constantly rained lightning bolts on his head. Three years ago her name was blackened in her hometown. She moved to New York, hoping to make a fresh start. But history was repeating itself.

She lifted her head. She would not give up. In a big city like New York there should be plenty of jobs. Of course she was blackballed in the theater district. No one who knew the name Ronda Starr would let her apply to mop the floors.

And how many offices boasted a piano? She loved playing for auditioning singers, and on the evenings she didn't have classes at the university, she stayed late at the office, holding her own private hymn-sing-along on the old upright. She was determined to earn her degree and make a career in music, if not as a performer, then as a teacher. She dashed away the tear that slid down her cheek. Crying wouldn't solve her problems.

She groped through the "if's," searching for a light at the end of the tunnel. If the police caught Rick, her name would be cleared. If she could talk to Mr. Rifkin, he might let her come back to her job. If wishes were horses...

The shrill ring of the phone brought her bolt upright. She stared at the instrument as though it were about to explode. *Please, don't let it be the police again.*

She let it ring four times before she picked up the receiver. She straightened her shoulders and put on her best office persona. "This is Tracy Dixon."

"Tracy? Thank goodness I reached you. It's Maggie."

"Maggie! What a surprise." Maggie O'Connor Scalia had been her closest friend in her hometown, ever since they were lab partners in ninth grade science class at Allerton High School. E-mail kept them in touch. Theirs was a forever friendship. But Tracy detected anguish in Maggie's voice, as though she were on the verge of tears. "Is something wrong?"

"I hate to tell you this—there's been a bad accident." Maggie paused.

Tracy's heart stopped. "Not Jeff," she whispered.

"Your brother is alive, but he's in critical condition. The paramedics took him to Jordan Hospital in Plymouth, but I think they moving him to a burn center in Boston. His doctors are trying to contact the family, but I couldn't find an address or phone number for your mother. Can you come home?"

Trying to catch her breath, Tracy clung to the receiver. She had made a solemn vow—under no circumstances would she return to Allerton again. But Jeff—Jeff was her only brother. She would give her life for him. The words were out of her mouth before she thought twice. "I'll be there as soon as I can."

She hung up the phone and stood dazed while a riot of thoughts trampled through her head. She had to leave a note for Heather, her roommate, but what should she say? She might be gone for days—or weeks—or months.

And Detective Diaz's warning echoed in her head. "Don't leave town." She had to let him know she was leaving. Surely the police didn't have the authority to keep her here in the city. They hadn't charged her with anything...yet. No matter. She had to go. Diaz would just have to wait and arrest her later.

****

Tracy's ancient Ford Galaxie gasped and wheezed as she pulled into her driveway. The two hundred mile trip from New York to Allerton was a major achievement for an old clunker that was about to celebrate its thirty-fifth birthday.

Everything was pitch black as she climbed out of her car. Swallowed up in the branches of a huge oak tree, the lone streetlight gave just enough illumination to reveal the weathered shingles on the old Cape Cod cottage. Two miles from town, with an apple orchard on one side and a cornfield on the other, the house wasn't within shouting distance of the nearest neighbor.

Although she had spent her entire childhood in this house, it seemed almost scary in the darkness. She prayed that Jeff had continued to pay the electric bill. When he returned from the war in Iraq, he began to drink heavily. Utility bills lost their meaning in the shadow of his depression.

Shivering in the biting cold air, she groped under the mat by the front door. As long as she could remember, the family kept an extra key there. Of course, a burglar would look there first. She never understood why the family bothered to lock the door at all. Her fingers closed around the key and noiselessly she let herself into the house. Throwing the switch by the door, she breathed a sigh of relief as light flooded the room.

It wasn't much warmer in the house than it was outside. She raised the switch on the thermostat, heartened by the sound of the heater roaring to life.

She felt as though she should tiptoe as she wandered through the lonely rooms. She was stepping back in time. The house was furnished in an assortment of styles and periods that Tracy called Early Thrift Shop. Everything smelled musty and unused. Nothing had been moved or changed in the three years since she left Allerton.

Six months ago her mother had fled Allerton, too, no longer able to endure the humiliation that her family had brought upon her good name. Tracy's father had disappeared in an alcoholic fog when she and Jeff were still in grade school. Her brother fell into the same alcoholic trap while the rumors about Tracy's reputation seemed to multiply. Now only Jeff remained in the house alone, living on his service disability pension and picking up odd jobs.

But this wasn't the time to stand here mourning the past. She needed to call Maggie and find out where Jeff was. She pulled her cell phone out of her purse. It was dead. In all the craziness of the past few days, she forgot to charge it. Crossing her fingers, she picked up the phone in the living room and heard the blessed sound of a dial tone.

She tried to swallow her disappointment when she reached a recording. "Scalia's Kennels," announced Maggie's cheerful voice. "Your dog's home away from home. Leave your name and phone number, and we'll get back to you as soon as possible."

There was nothing to do but leave a message.

Surveying the living room, she stopped to strike a few chords on the little spinet piano. As she expected, it was hopelessly out of tune.

She dropped wearily into an easy chair and then stifled a sneeze as she was enveloped in a cloud of dust. Apparently the house hadn't been cleaned since her mother left. She eyed the clock. Eight p.m. already. Surely Maggie would call back soon. The Scalias were probably just outside in the kennels.

She leaned her head back and closed her eyes. "Lord," she whispered, "please keep Jeff safe in your arms. He means more than life to me. Watch over him and give the doctors the wisdom to save him."

Waiting for Maggie's call was torture. She needed to do something—take some action. Should she call her mother? Faith Dixon had taken refuge with her sister Grace in St. Petersburg, Florida. Tracy could almost hear her mother's voice. "How did it happen? Was Jeff drunk? What will people say?" No, it would be better to wait and call when she knew more about her brother's condition.

Her stomach groaned for attention, and she realized she hadn't eaten a bite since gulping down a bowl of cereal at her apartment that morning. She pushed herself to her feet and headed for the kitchen. Maybe there would be something in the pantry besides a six pack of beer.

She opened the kitchen door and skidded to a dead stop. She was staring directly into the muzzle of a gun.

CHAPTER II

Paralyzed, Tracy could barely draw a breath. The gun was the size of a cannon. She was ready to meet God, but she would prefer to wait until another time. Her eyesight grew blurry as her legs turned to rubber.

And then the rumble of a deep voice penetrated the fog. "Hold it right there."

She dragged her gaze away from the gun and looked up. She made out the menacing figure of a man in a dark windbreaker and jeans. The room began to spin in dizzying circles. She was going to faint. She clutched at the doorjamb to keep the world from tipping over.

Through the haze, she saw him jam the pistol into its holster. Her knees crumbled, but he caught her before she hit the floor. As though she were a child, he swept her up in his arms. Barely conscious, she tried not to cling to his neck as he carried her back to the living room. Crushed against his broad chest, she was much too aware of the power in those wide shoulders. The muscular arms that gently eased her down onto the sofa could break her into little pieces.

She kept her eyes tightly closed, but sensed him looming over her. Was he trying to decide if he should put her out of her misery? And then she heard heavy footsteps as he strode out of the room.

Too weak and shaky to move, she clenched her

fists as the footsteps returned. Suddenly she felt the coolness of a damp cloth across her forehead. The wave of dizziness began to recede.

Clutching at the shredded remnants of her courage, she opened her eyes a crack. He was holding a small leather folder under her nose - a badge attached to an I.D. card. She made out the words "Leif Ericson, Chief of Police."

Police, she thought groggily. It didn't take them long to track me down.

Cautiously she studied her captor. Leif Ericson. Right out of the history books. He definitely looked like a Viking with that rough-hewn face, powerful build, tawny hair, and eyes the color of a stormy ocean. His five o'clock shadow looked more like seven o'clock or eight, which only enhanced the image. A helmet with horns would complete the picture.

Should she be relieved that she wasn't about to be shot or fearful that he would drag her back to New York before she had a chance to see Jeff?

Peering up at him, she thought she caught a glimpse of concern. "I've never fainted in my entire life," she whispered.

"A Smith and Wesson has that effect on people," he growled. He snatched the ladderback chair away from the desk, placed it backward in front of her, and then straddled it with his arms across the top rung.

The concern she had seen just a moment before had vanished, replaced by a scowl of suspicion. A storm brewed in those sea-gray eyes. Deliberately he invaded her space.

"If you tell me that you broke into this house to get warm, I'm not going to believe you. So why don't you tell me what you are doing here."

Tracy gaped at him. *What am I doing here? I'm minding my own business in my own house. When did that become a crime?*

She struggled to a sitting position, lifting her

chin in defiance. "I'm Tracy Dixon, and this is my home." She paused. "I mean it's my mother's home. Well, actually it's my brother's home." *He must think I'm a raving lunatic.*

"Dixon!" He eyed her with disbelief. "You're Tracy Dixon?" He glared at her as though he expected her nose to start growing.

Tracy didn't know why she was on the defensive. She should be the one giving him the third degree. "I'm trying to find out where my brother is. He's been badly injured in an accident."

"How did you hear about the accident?" The Viking snapped the question like a whip.

"My friend Maggie Scalia called me. I don't understand why there's a problem here."

"So you came home to see your brother?"

Tracy merely nodded. She should have added, That's the only reason I would set foot in Allerton again.

"And your mother. Where is she?"

"My mother moved to Florida. She left the house for Jeff to use."

"So you're just visiting?"

"Just visiting," she echoed.

After a long pause, the Viking stood up. He swung his chair back into place at the desk and announced calmly, "They moved Jeff to the burn center at Mass. General in Boston today." He headed for the door and then turned. "I saw the lights in the house and thought there was an intruder. I'm sorry to have frightened you, Miss Dixon."

Tracy sat open-mouthed, watching him leave. So, the NYPD didn't send him. Apparently he had no clue that she was under suspicion in the jewelry theft.

Propping herself up on her elbows, she held her breath until she caught the sound of an engine roaring to life. He came in to investigate the lights in the house, but how had he gained entry? Her nerves couldn't take another home invasion. If she stayed here any length of time, she would have to do something about the locks on the doors.

"Leif Ericson." She whispered the name under her breath. If he weren't so scary, he would be a good-looking man. And if he ever cracked a smile, he'd be downright gorgeous. Not that she was looking for romance. The men in her life had given her nothing but trouble and betrayal. Sometimes she pictured a big "Kick Me" sign pinned to her back. And police officers meant double trouble. Leif Ericson was just one big complication. She came home to see her brother, and no Neanderthal with a badge was going to stop her.

****

Leif maneuvered his SUV into the parking lot behind the one-story brick building which the Allerton police shared with the fire department. He had discovered that being police chief in a small town involved more than burglaries and accidents. Today included breakfast at the Elk's Club, explaining why the police department needed to upgrade its computer programs. Allerton was at least five years behind the rest of the state. He was struggling to drag the town, kicking and screaming, into the twenty-first century.

He limped up the steps to the back door to find Lucille on the phone, as usual. She was his dispatcher as well as his clerk, computer nerd, and right hand. The headset was as much a part of her hairdo as the prim bun of gray hair at the back of her neck.

He inherited Lucille along with his office when he accepted the job of police chief six months ago. She was probably eighty years old, but he didn't dare to ask. Some old timers in town insisted that Lucille waited on Plymouth Rock to welcome the Pilgrims when they stepped off the Mayflower.

"Leland," she greeted him. "There's a detective

on the phone calling from New York." Lucille was the only person in town who dared to call him by his given name.

"Thanks, I'll take it in my office." Leif closed the door behind him and settled at his desk. New York, he puzzled, picking up the phone. He didn't think a New Yorker could find Allerton on the map.

"Chief Ericson here," he said briskly.

"Chief, this is Detective Diaz, NYPD. We need your assistance."

"Glad to help. What can we do for you?"

The detective's voice sounded like coarse sandpaper. "You've probably heard about the theft of jewelry from Ronda Starr's home."

"It made all the papers here."

"We're trying to trace the whereabouts of the suspect, Rick Timmons."

Leif came to full alert. "Do you have reason to believe he's in this area?"

"I've been questioning a young woman named Tracy Dixon who attended Ronda Starr's reception with Timmons. She nearly convinced me that she was an innocent dupe, but now she's skipped town. She left me a message with some cockamamie story about her brother in Allerton having an accident."

"Tracy Dixon," Leif muttered. *What a dim bulb I am.* He was probably the only one in Allerton who didn't make the connection between his Tracy Dixon and the woman in the news articles about the theft.

"She told you the truth about the accident, Detective Diaz. Her brother is in the burn unit at Massachusetts General."

Diaz sounded skeptical. "Well, maybe she is on the level, but she picked an interesting time to leave New York."

"So, how can we help you?"

"Keep an eye out for Rick Timmons. If Miss Dixon was his accomplice, he may try to contact her."

Leif picked up his pen and a notepad. "Give me a description. Do you have a picture?"

"No, apparently he's an old pro. He knows how to blend into the wallpaper, but I'll fax all the information we have. He's well built, about 6'2", blond hair, brown eyes, clean-shaven. He has probably changed his name and his appearance, but he should be easy to spot in a small town. If Miss Dixon has a visitor, you'll know what to look for."

"I'll get the word to my men," Leif assured him.

"Better warn them this guy is vicious," Diaz added. "We still don't know if the butler is going to live. Timmons used the butt of a pistol to beat him senseless. It looks as though the butler caught him in the act of cracking Miss Starr's safe."

"Do you have a description of the stolen jewelry?"

"I'll fax you a list. The street value is probably at least a half million, but most of the pieces are irreplaceable—family heirlooms, gifts from celebrities, stuff like that. Priceless."

"I'm on it. I'll stay in touch." Leif jotted down the detective's phone number and sank back in his chair. Massaging his bad knee, he considered his strategy. The public tended to think a crime wave in a small town involved someone spitting on the sidewalk. But this was grand theft and attempted murder, and Tracy Dixon was right in the middle of it.

He found it hard to believe that someone who looked like a fairy tale princess was aiding and abetting a dangerous criminal. When he questioned Tracy, he managed to maintain his professional demeanor, suppressing his normal male weakness for a pretty face, but it wasn't easy to keep his focus in the depths of those beautiful eyes. They were a startling clear blue with a thick fringe of dark lashes. And, when he picked her up, he had almost lost his objectivity. She was slender, but her curves were in all the right places. A police officer tried to cultivate his powers of observation, but maybe he had noticed a little too much about the lovely Miss Dixon.

A year ago, he let a beautiful face undermine his good judgment, and he paid the price for his weakness. He wasn't about to make the same mistake again. Miss Tracy Dixon was about to acquire an extra shadow.

****

Armed with a map of Boston, Tracy climbed into her car. It was much warmer today. The sun shone bright in the clear blue sky, and a light breeze from the east brought the scent of salt air from the bay. The beautiful spring day gave a lift to her spirits.

Maggie had given her a little more information about Jeff's accident. Witnesses said he had been driving at a high rate of speed, weaving in and out of traffic on Route 3, when he spun out of control, plunged off the highway, and plowed into a tree. In an instant the car was engulfed in flames. A few brave souls risked their lives to pull Jeff out of the inferno, but not before he was badly burned.

From her earliest years Tracy adored her big brother. Growing up with no close neighbors, they turned to each other—the two musketeers. When Jeff became the man of the family at age ten, he became her protector. No one dared to give his sister a hard time. He was her superhero.

She whispered a prayer. "Lord, thank you for those wonderful people who saved Jeff's life. He's been hiding from you, but he needs you now. Keep watching over him." And then she added a postscript. "Please, I want him to know I'm here for him."

She backed out of the driveway and headed for town. Unfortunately she had to pass through the center of Allerton to get to the interstate. By now, everyone had probably heard the news of her latest misadventures. She was sure she heard a car driving slowly past her house several times during the night. Maybe nosy neighbors, but she suspected the police chief had put her under surveillance.

She felt a tug of nostalgia as she braked for the stoplight at Main Street. Keith Bradford had smeared her name all over town, but no matter what her reputation in Allerton, it was home. As far as she knew, the residents who pitied her outnumbered the ones who looked down their noses. Of course, she wasn't sure which was worse—pity or disdain.

The center of town looked the same, as though it were caught in a time warp. The tall white spire of the community church looked out like a benevolent monarch over the buildings that surrounded the village green—the massive town hall, the gracious eighteenth century homes, and the inevitable antique shops. Walden's drugstore was still on the corner, looking just as it did when she and Maggie had made their regular stop for a soda after choir practice each week.

As the light changed, she came out of her reverie and accelerated into the intersection. Crack! A deafening explosion of sound blasted her eardrums. She slammed on the brakes. Was someone shooting at her? She ducked down behind the steering wheel, waiting for the next shot. But everything was quiet.

Cautiously she lifted her head and peered out the window. The noise had attracted a few spectators, but they didn't seem frightened, just curious. Perhaps it was just a blowout. Her tire treads were getting thin.

She couldn't just sit here in the middle of Main Street. Deciding she wasn't under attack, she climbed out of the car. But a close inspection showed her tires were intact.

Mr. Walden, the elderly pharmacist, waved at her. "Do you want me to call a tow truck, Tracy?"

"I'm OK," Tracy assured him. "I'll just drive down to Henry's garage and have him take a look at it."

The old man made a wry face. "Honey, you won't be driving anywhere. You just threw a rod. From the sound of it, I'd say it went right through the engine block."

Tracy gaped at him in disbelief. She needed her car. She couldn't wait another day for repairs. She had to get to Boston now—today.

"What's the problem here?"

Tracy spun around, almost relieved to see the police chief striding toward her. He was in uniform today, clean shaven, looking very official, very competent, and very much in charge. She wanted to throw up her hands and burst into tears, but she refused to cry in front of her hometown audience. "Mr. Walden says I've thrown a rod," she managed.

Without a word he slid into the driver's seat of her car and turned the key in the ignition. The racket that followed sounded like a dozen machine guns all firing at once. Quickly he switched off the motor. Stepping out, he crouched down to peer under the car. Tracy stared at the puddle of oil seeping out into the street.

Leif got to his feet, shaking his head. "Sorry, Miss Dixon, it's definitely a blown rod."

Tracy knew as much about the anatomy of an automobile as she did about the space shuttle, but from the expression on his face she knew she had a major problem. "I suppose it will take quite a while to fix that," she said wistfully.

Leif was decent enough not to laugh at her ignorance. He actually looked sympathetic as he loomed over her. "Miss Dixon, it could take Henry a week or more to find parts for that car. And even if he can track down an engine, are you sure it's worth the expense to repair a car as old as that one? It's going to set you back at least two thousand dollars. You could sell it to one of those antique car buffs who like to restore old automobiles."

Tracy spirits hit bottom as she stared at the old Ford. When her mother moved away, she left the car for Tracy to use, but it cost quite a bit to park in the lot at her Brooklyn apartment. She had been ready to sell the Galaxie or even give it away. Public transportation in New York was cheap and convenient, but as long as she was stuck here in Allerton, she had to have wheels. She considered herself competent to handle anything that came her way, but now she was totally at a loss. She couldn't afford repairs. She couldn't afford a used car. She couldn't even afford a rental.

"I need to get to Boston to see Jeff—today." Tracy could hear the quaver in her own voice.

Leif nodded. "OK, we'll fix you up with a tow, and then I'll take you to the hospital."

"No. Oh, no," she protested. She had already spent too much time in the company of the chief of police. "No, I couldn't ask you to do that. If you would just take me to Plymouth, maybe I can catch the train."

"You didn't ask. I offered. I'm taking you to Boston." His offer sounded suspiciously like an order.

But she had no choice. All her plans to keep a low profile vanished in a cloud of exhaust. If she kept protesting, she'd just give him more reason to be suspicious of her. She choked out a feeble, "Thanks."

Here we go again. She heaved a weary sigh. *So much for avoiding the police.*

CHAPTER III

Leif eased his SUV into the flow of traffic on the interstate. With rush hour over, it should be an easy ride into Boston. No ice slicks today. The world was starting to turn green again. Maybe winter would finally give up.

He caught the scent of Tracy's perfume. He was no authority on perfumes, but she smelled like spring flowers. Everything about her baffled him. Her sweetness and innocence just didn't fit the typical criminal profile. But he couldn't let that influence him. He had learned his lesson. Tracy wouldn't be the first woman to be led astray by a slick, fast-talking boyfriend.

He slanted a quick glance at his passenger. She seemed unusually subdued, huddled against the door, staring out at the trees. Of course, she wasn't too thrilled when he virtually kidnapped her this morning. She probably felt as though she were under arrest.

And she was dealing with some tough issues. Her brother's life was in jeopardy, her car was a disaster, and the NYPD was breathing down her neck. Which was uppermost in her mind?

He had been debating the best way to keep her under surveillance when that blown rod dropped her right into his lap. This was his chance to dig out a little more information about her relationship with Rick Timmons.

Several of Allerton's upstanding citizens hinted that Tracy Dixon wasn't the innocent she appeared to be. He pressed them for specifics, but nobody gave him anything concrete.

Others suggested that you couldn't expect Tracy to be a model citizen. After all, her father deserted the family when she and Jeff were just kids, and her mother was one of those fluttery, helpless types. The grandparents had to support the family.

In any event his pure-as-snow princess apparently was hiding some dirty laundry. He would just have to dig deeper to find the secrets hidden behind that perfect façade.

"So, you're a celebrity. Made all the headlines."

Fire blazed in those brilliant blue eyes as she turned to face him. She had a way of lifting her chin that said, "Don't tread on me." But was that sudden flush in her cheeks a sign of guilt or anger?

"The newspapers don't tell the whole story." She shook her head. "I was so gullible. Rick Timmons used me to get into Miss Starr's house. No one would have suspected he was planning a robbery."

"Did you date him often?" Leif didn't know why that thought bothered him.

She sat up straighter in her seat as though she were ready for battle. "I never dated Rick. The few times I ran into him I was at a restaurant with a group of friends. We were never alone together. The night of the reception we were just sharing the cost of a cab."

"Why not drive your own car?"

Tracy made a face. "It's impossible to find a parking space in Manhattan."

"So, do you have a boyfriend in New York?" Leif was surprised to hear the question come out of his mouth. It had nothing to do with the robbery.

She seemed to relax a bit. She looked relieved to drop the subject of Timmons. "I dated a little. Nobody special."

"Anybody special in Allerton?" he probed. *What's my problem? I'm supposed to be investigating a crime, not analyzing her love life.*

But the blush returned to her cheeks. He had touched a sore spot. There was someone special in Allerton—or there had been—and she wasn't happy about it. Her face revealed too much.

But she simply answered, "No." She didn't offer any details.

Leif drove in silence for a moment. He needed to get his line of questioning back on track. The crime was the jewel theft, not a long-lost lover.

"So, you went off to New York to take Broadway by storm." He sensed her hesitation before she answered.

"Not really. I just wanted to see what life was like in the big city."

Was that the real reason she left Allerton? Something in her voice hinted that there was a lot more to the story.

"The newspapers said you were an aspiring actress."

She wrinkled her nose. "Reporters like to dramatize everything. I don't think I'm the Broadway type. All I want is to finish earning my degree in music. I didn't even think about Broadway until I got a job in an agent's office. Then my roommate started nagging me to try out for a musical. I sing a little."

"Really? The church always welcomes another voice in the choir."

Tears welled up in her eyes. "I—I don't know how long—how long I'll be here. I mean—everything is so mixed up right now. I couldn't..." She trailed off into silence.

"Because of Jeff?" He finished her thought.

"I can't think about anything else. I'm anxious to see him, but I'm afraid—afraid to find out how badly he's injured—afraid that he's scarred for life—afraid that he's not going to live through this." She made an attempt to brush away the tears. "I'm just sorry I had to impose on you."

She looked so dispirited, he felt like a schoolyard bully. "You're not imposing on me. I wanted to check on Jeff myself. We've become pretty close friends."

"Close friends!" Her eyes widened. "You and Jeff?"

"He's been coming to church with me."

"Jeff went to church?"

She couldn't have looked more stunned if he had hit her over the head with his night stick. She sat there speechless, gazing at him in disbelief. This probably wasn't the best time to burden her with more sad details about Jeff's life. It would only make her feel worse if she knew what Jeff was doing just twenty-four hours before the accident.

They were in the heart of Boston. It was time to leave the interstate and join the traffic on the city streets. He glanced across at his passenger as he turned the SUV down the exit ramp toward the hospital. All the color had drained from Tracy's face.

****

Tracy fidgeted on the hard bench, clutching her purse to steady her trembling hands. The nurse in the burn unit said the doctor wanted to talk to her before she visited Jeff. Leif sat stoically beside her, a mountain of patience. She couldn't read the thoughts behind that rugged face, but there was something comforting about his solid presence.

She jumped to her feet when a tall man in a dark business suit approached. He looked more like a corporate executive than a physician. "Miss Dixon?" he asked, extending his hand. "I'm Dr. Burrows."

Her heart raced. "Jeff?" she whispered. "How is he? Can I see him?"

"I have to be honest with you. At this point Mr. Dixon's prognosis is bleak. His condition is extremely critical. Now, for the first seventy-two hours, we're in the resuscitation phase. So far he's holding his own, but you need to know that we're keeping him in a drug-induced coma." In spite of his professional manner, the doctor had kind eyes and a gentle voice.

"He's in a coma?" The world crashed down around her. "Then he can't talk to me."

"Miss Dixon, he suffered second and third degree burns over seventy percent of his body. It will be several weeks before we can even begin to reduce the sedation. Tomorrow we'll start the skin grafts. Mr. Dixon won't be out of danger until we can close his wounds. This will be a long, slow process."

"But can I see him?" Tracy pleaded. None of this would seem real until she saw Jeff with her own eyes.

"Right now the greatest danger is infection. You can observe him through the glass. Even if you go inside and talk to him, I doubt that he would hear you or even know that you were there. You should be prepared for his appearance. We've infused his body with an extraordinary amount of fluid to replace the loss through his wounds. You'll notice a great deal of swelling."

Tracy still couldn't bring herself to believe they were having this conversation. Jeff, in a coma, burned over seventy percent of his body.

But the doctor continued, "We're doing everything possible to ease his suffering. There's a ventilator to support his breathing, of course, and a feeding tube in his nose."

"Of course," Tracy echoed helplessly.

"If you'll wait here a moment, I'll have someone escort you to his room."

"Am I allowed to go?" Leif asked. "I'm not family—just a close friend."

The doctor nodded. "I'll call the nurse."

In minutes the nurse signaled them to follow

her. Leif limped along behind Tracy, wondering if she could handle the shock of seeing her brother's condition. She looked so pale and wobbly.

He breathed the acrid smell of disinfectant as the nurse led them through the sterile corridors. She stopped at a glass-walled room. Leif choked back a gasp. In spite of the doctor's warning, he wasn't prepared for the sight of his friend. Jeff's face was swollen beyond recognition. The tubes and wires and bandages obscured Leif's view, but it looked as though Jeff's eyebrows had been burned off and his hair was charred. The rest of his body was draped in white sheets. It was impossible to estimate the extent of the damage. How on earth could anyone survive that trauma?

Leif studied the screens above and beside Jeff's bed. They were monitoring his vital signs—his blood pressure and heart rate. He tried to make sense of the numbers. And then he realized that Tracy was clutching his arm, clinging to him as though she were drowning. She seemed to be in a trance, just staring at her brother with a flood of tears rolling down her cheeks.

Leif hesitated for less than a heartbeat before pulling her into his arms. She sobbed out her grief on his shoulder.

****

Tracy sank back in her seat in the SUV. A blinding headache pounded nails into her skull. Even in her worst nightmares she couldn't imagine anything more frightening than this.

She felt the touch of Leif's hand on her shoulder, offering comfort. "He's in good hands, Tracy. They'll pull him through."

She had to cling to that hope. They drove in silence heading back to Allerton. She was grateful that Leif didn't feel the need to indulge in idle chatter. She closed her eyes to shut out the world. She wasn't ready to deal with anything but thoughts of Jeff. Against her closed eyelids she pictured that swollen face and the tangle of tubes and hoses that were keeping him alive. If the nurse hadn't led them to his room, she could never have identified her own brother.

It wasn't supposed to be this way. Jeff Dixon had been Allerton's shining star. Everyone predicted great things in store for him. He was bright and athletic and handsome. She'd been heartsick when he dropped out of college to enlist in the army.

And then he came home from Iraq with half his right leg missing. The injuries drained away all the life and sparkle from his personality. Despite her vows to stay away from Allerton, she came back from New York to celebrate his return home and to help him get settled in while the rest of the town presented their hero with the keys to a brand new car fitted to accommodate his injuries.

He was offered a choice of a dozen different jobs, but he had lost all interest in living. He spurned the job offers and sought refuge in a bottle. Refusing to wear his prosthesis, he sat day after day, staring at the television screen without knowing what he was watching. She prayed fervently that he would shake off his depression, but he seemed satisfied to function in the role of town drunk.

Leif stunned her this morning when he said her brother had been going to church. She had phoned Jeff and written long letters from New York, urging him to attend church, but he ignored her pleas.

Leif walked with a limp. Maybe their disabilities had forged a bond between the two men.

She turned to study Leif's face. There was such quiet strength in those chiseled features. "Please pray for Jeff," she whispered.

Leif's face softened. "Believe me, I've been praying for him constantly."

"But Jeff turned his back on God. Do you think He really cares what happens to Jeff?"

"I believe God never stops caring for his children, no matter what they've done." Leif spoke without hesitation. "And Jeff was finding his way back to God again."

His words reassured her, and yet it was so bitterly ironic—just when Jeff was taking his first steps back, the world exploded in his face.

She smothered a dreary sigh. Now she had to make a decision—go back to New York and look for work, or stick it out here in Allerton. If she were in the city and Jeff's condition changed—for better or for worse—she needed to be here.

But there was the matter of money. She would have to find a job. Allerton was not the hub of the universe. And if she were lucky enough to find something, it meant a two-mile walk into town until her car was repaired. The auto insurance didn't cover a rental. On top of everything else, she was still responsible for half the rent on her apartment in Brooklyn. She wouldn't consider sticking her roommate with paying the whole cost. If she decided to stay in Allerton, she would have to tell Heather to find another roommate. But what if Detective Diaz didn't give her a choice? Maybe he'd force her to return to New York. The pounding in her head was building to a crescendo.

She opened her eyes, startled as Leif pulled the car to the side of the road. She realized they had left the interstate and were just a few miles from home. She watched in silence as he punched the numbers on his cell phone.

"Hey, Mark," he said, "how about calling Mrs. Davis and see if she can pick you guys up for baseball practice. I'm running a little late."

He paused. "Good boy. Tell Luke to go easy on that ankle. He should wear his high tops. I'll be there as soon as I can." He switched off the phone and put the car back into motion.

Tracy kept her eyes focused on the road, but she

found herself thinking about Leif, instead of Jeff. So the chief had children. He was probably a great father. She wondered if there was a Mrs. Leif—not that it mattered to her. She was tempted to ask, but she had made herself a solemn promise—no more involvement with the police. She cried all over Leif's uniform today, and that was enough.

Guilt nibbled at the fringes of her conscience as she realized he had put aside his own plans for the day to chauffeur her into Boston. "I've made you late," she apologized.

"No sweat. The Davises won't mind picking up the boys. I've hauled their kids all over town many times."

She had rewarded Leif's kindness today with the silent treatment most of the way back from Boston. She groped for something—anything—to say. "Did Luke hurt his ankle?"

For the first time since she met him, Leif smiled. That smile transformed his whole face. His eyes crinkled and deep creases in his cheeks bracketed his mouth. He was gorgeous when he smiled.

"It's just a slight sprain. Luke is always among the walking wounded. He's a disaster magnet."

She heard the pride and affection in his voice as he talked about the boy.

"How about Mark?"

"Mark is so well coordinated, I have to wonder how those two could possibly be brothers."

Tracy tried to think of something else to say, but she was wrung dry. She needed to stop for groceries, but there was no way she would ask Leif for another favor today. Maybe Maggie could take her to the store in the morning.

She was lost in her thoughts until Leif brought the car to a stop in her driveway. She managed to dredge up her good manners. "Thanks so much for taking me to the hospital. Seeing Jeff in that condition was hard to take, but ..." She had to admit it. "But having you there helped a lot."

"Any time," he offered.

His gaze fastened on her face. Was he trying to read her mind? That relentless stare was like an X-ray.

And he didn't rush away. He waited while she picked up the mail and unlocked the front door. She waved as he pulled away and then stood watching as his SUV disappeared. She should be relieved that she was finally out of the clutches of the law, but she felt a small twinge of regret. There was something about Leif Ericson. He radiated an aura of strength and dependability. She hoped his children knew how lucky they were.

But she would be making a serious mistake to lean on the police chief. His chivalry today was out of his concern for Jeff. Jeff's sister was an entirely different matter. To Leif, Tracy Dixon was just another face on a "Wanted" poster.

CHAPTER IV

Maggie Scalia sat sipping a cup of coffee at the kitchen table while Tracy stowed away her groceries. Last night, in spite of her exhaustion, Tracy had scrubbed the kitchen clean. The shabby curtains needed to be replaced, but that would have to wait. She hoped her old friend would ignore the layers of dust throughout the rest of the house. She vowed to spend the next few days scouring the place from top to bottom.

A visit with Maggie always lifted her spirits. Standing six foot tall with a head of flaming red hair and a temper to match, Maggie proudly lived up to her nickname, "The Towering Inferno." With Tracy standing just five foot four, the townspeople labeled them Mutt and Jeff.

They had done a lot of reminiscing as they made the round trip to the grocery store. Tracy found herself smiling at some of those memories.

For a brief moment at the store, she experienced the eerie sensation that she was being followed. But Maggie's chatter brushed away the cobwebs of paranoia. If someone was watching her, it had to be one of Leif Ericson's men waiting to see what she planned to steal next.

"Have you called your mother yet?" Maggie asked.

Tracy closed the refrigerator and leaned against the door. "I called her last night. She's so upset about Jeff, she wants to get on a plane and come right home. But Aunt Grace is having triple bypass surgery. I convinced Mom to stay there and take care of her sister. We can all pray for Jeff wherever we are, but the only humans who can do anything for him are the doctors."

With the groceries in place, Tracy poured herself a cup of coffee and took a seat at the table.

Maggie eyed her curiously. "There's something else bothering you."

Maggie knew her too well. Tracy hated to unload her troubles on her friend, but the problems were coming thick and fast. She waved at the thick wad of letters and bills tucked haphazardly into a paper napkin holder.

"Maggie, I'm really scared. I looked through all these utility bills—the electric, the gas, the phone, the water. They all show the amount of the charges, but they are marked 'Do Not Pay.' Jeff must have some kind of automatic payment system with the bank."

Maggie raised an eyebrow. "That doesn't sound too scary."

"I wish. I'm sure Jeff thought he had taken care of everything, so he ignored the bills as they came in." Tracy picked up one of the papers, holding it by two fingers as though it were in danger of bursting into flame. "This arrived yesterday." She pushed an official looking notice across the table. It was a communication from the town of Allerton.

Maggie studied the notice and then looked up in shock. "His property taxes! They're supposed to be paid quarterly, but he hasn't made a payment for over a year!"

Tracy heaved a deep sigh. "If I know Jeff, he never even looked at the tax bills. He just stuffed the notices here with the other bills and forgot about them."

Maggie jumped up and paced a circle around the

room. "Tracy, you know the town can seize the house and put it up for auction if the property taxes aren't paid."

A sharp stab of pain told Tracy her headache was coming back. "I know, Mag, but what can I do? I don't have five thousand dollars, and that's miles over the limit on my credit card. I can check Jeff's bank statements. He might have enough money in his savings account to pay these taxes. But even then, I can't touch his accounts while he's in a coma."

Maggie was determined to find a solution. She made another circle around the kitchen. "What about your mother?"

"Mom's living on a small inheritance from my grandparents, but that's all the money she has until she's eligible for social security."

"There has to be some way you can legally get access to Jeff's money." Maggie sat down at the table again, chewing on her lip. "Why don't you ask Keith?"

Speechless, Tracy could only stare at her.

"Keith would know what to do," Maggie insisted.

"Keith Bradford!" Tracy groaned. "Please tell me you're kidding. Can't you see his knife still sticking out of my back?"

"That's just the point," Maggie said triumphantly. "You'd have to pay another lawyer, but Keith owes you—big time. He knows how to obtain power of attorney or whatever authority you need."

"I would have to be at the end of my rope to ask Keith Bradford for the time of day." *But I am at the end of my rope and barely hanging onto the last threads.*

****

Leif pulled a chair up to Lucille's desk and waited for her to finish her phone call. She was trying to soothe an irate citizen whose garbage had not been picked up. The problem should have been reported to the town hall, but the residents of Allerton considered Lucille the town's central information guru. Leif wondered when the local school kids would start phoning in their homework questions.

"Yes, Leland?" She looked up, pushing back the earphones on her headset.

Lucille was not a gossip, but she knew everything that had ever happened in Allerton. He had to talk fast to catch her between calls. "Tell me about Tracy Dixon."

Lucille frowned, bringing more creases to her wrinkled cheeks. "I suppose you've been listening to all those rumors."

Leif nodded. "So give me the facts."

"Well, about that shoplifting charge ..."

The phone rang and Leif ground his teeth with impatience while Lucille dispatched an officer to round up a stray cow.

Lucille finished her call and continued her story. "When Tracy was a senior in high school, she was checking out at one of those music stores in Brockton. The clerk put her purchases in a bag, but the manager noticed several CD's sticking out of her jacket pocket. He stopped her and held her until the police came. Tracy swore she had no idea how the CD's got into her pocket, but she couldn't convince the store manager, the police or the judge. The juvenile court sentenced her to two weeks of community service."

"Did you believe her?" Leif considered Lucille a sharp judge of character.

"Tracy Dixon wouldn't steal a postage stamp. That sneaky Skip Martin was in the shop with her. You can bet he was the one who slipped those CD's into Tracy's pocket. But the police had already decided that Tracy was the culprit. They never even bothered to question Skip."

The phone rang again and Leif sat back with a groan. At this rate it he'd need a week to get the details of Tracy's past.

Lucille dealt with two more phone calls before she continued. "And those rumors you've heard about Tracy's character are all Keith Bradford's doing. Did you know Tracy and Keith were engaged to be married?"

"Keith Bradford, the state representative?" Bradford was Allerton's leading citizen.

Lucille nodded. "Tracy was in college when he put the ring on her finger. Keith was on the town's board of selectmen at the time, but he decided to run for the state legislature. Naturally Tracy became his strongest supporter. She spent every spare minute working for his campaign—calling voters, putting up posters, stuffing envelopes, you name it.

"But the minute Keith won the election, he dumped Tracy. Everyone thought he was a heel for breaking the engagement, so he started dropping hints that Tracy had been involved in some shady activities in the past. He pretended that he was too much of a gentleman to reveal her deep, dark secrets, but he let everyone know that a woman of Tracy's character wasn't an appropriate wife for a state representative."

"Did Tracy deny the rumors?"

"She challenged him to tell the world one single thing she had done, but Keith was a smart politician. His only answer was that knowing smirk."

Leif still wasn't convinced that Tracy was an innocent lamb. Bradford must have known something. "So you think there was nothing to the rumors Bradford was spreading?"

"I don't believe a word of it. But people love a scandal, and there were plenty of folks who jumped on Keith's bandwagon. But the final blow for Tracy was when the announcement came out in the paper that Keith was marrying Louise Lawrence, the governor's daughter."

"Louise Bradford is the governor's daughter?" Leif was caught off balance. He still had a lot to learn about the good citizens of Allerton.

Lucille nodded. "Louise is a lovely person, but all Keith cares about is her political connections. Anyway, a week before Keith's wedding, Tracy packed her bags and moved to New York."

"So what about this latest business with Ronda Starr?"

"If Tracy said she wasn't involved, she wasn't involved."

The phone rang again and Leif got to his feet. "Thanks, Lucille. I get the picture." He turned back to his office, trying to absorb all these new details. Normally he had complete faith in Lucille's judgment, but he tended to believe in the old adage, where there's smoke, there's fire. And there was enough smoke swirling around Tracy Dixon to signal a four-alarm blaze. Her murky past sounded like the perfect background for an accessory to Rick Timmons and the theft of Ronda Starr's jewelry.

****

Tracy stood at the door to Keith Bradford's law office without making a move to ring the bell. The old colonial house was still Keith's home, but he had added a side entrance for his office. A small brass plate on the door stated, "Keith A. Bradford, Attorney at Law." She wouldn't have been surprised to see a flashing neon sign proclaiming, "Keith A. Bradford, Distinguished State Representative."

And then it came again—that eerie sensation that sent prickles down her spine. She was being watched—someone was following her. Heart pounding, she spun around, but the ghosts had vanished. All she could see was a group of children, laughing and shouting as they played tag on the village green. Yes, she really was paranoid.

Every muscle in her body knotted with tension.

Facing Keith again was going to be torture, but Maggie hadn't given her a choice. Maggie made the appointment for her and then insisted on driving her into town.

Tracy had not packed much of a wardrobe for her trip home, but her dark plaid skirt and navy blazer looked reasonably business-like. Go ahead. Ring the bell. Let's get this over with.

A pretty little blond answered the buzzer. Her heavy eye makeup gave her the appearance of a startled raccoon. "Miss Dixon," she said politely. "Please come in. Mr. Bradford will be with you in just a minute."

The receptionist returned to her desk where the nameplate read "Susan Collins." The waiting room was furnished in Early American style, attractive, but unpretentious. Tracy sank into a comfortable chair. Her nerves were jangling, but she tried to project an aura of ease and confidence. As she reached for a magazine, Keith made his appearance.

"Tracy, it's so good to see you again." He oozed the famous Bradford charm from every pore. He hadn't changed much over the past three years. Keith was still a handsome man although his sandy hair was getting a little thinner and his waistline a little thicker.

As Tracy stood, he came across the room, clearly intending to give her a hug. She quickly extended her hand, limiting him to a cool handshake, but he took a little too long to release his grasp.

"Come in, come in," he urged. Tracy bristled at the possessive touch of his hand on her back as he guided her into his office.

He took his seat behind a large mahogany desk and waved her to the chair opposite him. "It's been a long time. You're looking great." His eyes appraised every detail of her appearance.

"Thank you." Tracy gritted her teeth. This meeting was supposed to be strictly impersonal.

Stalling a moment to gather her wits, she gazed around the office. Typical Keith—an impressive assortment of framed degrees and certificates on the paneled walls and rows of bookshelves crammed with heavy legal tomes.

"Now, what can I do for you?" His smile was almost a leer.

She reached across the desk to place the tax notice in front of him. "I'm sure you know about Jeff's accident. He's in the burn center at Mass. General. He's so badly burned that they have to keep him in a coma for weeks. I've looked through his bank statements. Jeff has enough money in his savings to pay these taxes, but I need some authority to access his account."

To Tracy's relief, Keith's manner became all business. "That shouldn't be a problem," he said confidently. "We'll petition the probate court to have you named as conservator of your brother's assets. That will give you responsibility for managing his assets and using them for his benefit."

He turned to the filing cabinet behind his desk and pulled out a printed document. "We can take care of the application right now."

It took just a few minutes to fill in the blanks on the form. Tracy felt the knots of tension beginning to unravel. "The taxes are so long overdue, I'm really afraid that the town will take his house. How long will it take for the judge to approve my petition?"

Keith steepled his hands and peered over them, his face solemn. "Well, there's some red tape involved. It might take several weeks. But the judge will appoint a temporary conservator, someone the judge knows and trusts, to deal with Jeff's immediate needs. He'll also appoint a guardian ad litem to conduct a full investigation of your qualifications. The judge won't appoint you as conservator until the guardian ad litem makes his report, either recommending your appointment or not."

Tracy's anxiety level shot up to the top of the meter. With her reputation, a judge would never consider approving her petition to handle her brother's money. "What happens if the guardian doesn't recommend my appointment?"

Keith didn't appear concerned. "Well, the immediate problem is payment of the property taxes. The temporary conservator can take care of that. Then it will be time to address the matter of your appointment to take over as conservator."

"How can I find out who has been named temporary conservator? He'll need to see the tax bill right away."

"I should know within a week." And then Keith's all-business demeanor disappeared. He was Prince Charming again. His voice took on an intimate tone. "Maybe the judge will appoint me temporary conservator. We could spend some quality time together reviewing Jeff's situation." He emphasized the word "quality" with a suggestive lift of an eyebrow.

Tracy didn't respond. She did not want to spend one "quality" minute in the company of Keith Bradford. She pushed back her chair and surged to her feet.

Before she turned away, Keith circled his desk. He put an arm around her and pulled her closer. "Tracy," he purred, "we made a good team. You know you're the only woman I ever really cared for. Marrying Louise was just political strategy."

Tracy was trembling from head to toe. Furious, she pulled away from his touch and stared at him in disbelief. Did he think that by coming to him for legal advice she was issuing a subtle invitation to rekindle their relationship? Had he forgotten that he had humiliated her and smeared her name before the whole town of Allerton?

But she needed his help. She clenched her fists,

keeping a tight hold on her rage. "Whatever your reasons, Keith, you are a married man. Please call me as soon as you know the name of the temporary conservator." Shoulders squared, she turned and left his office, stifling the urge to slam the door.

CHAPTER V

Maggie brought her dusty blue pickup truck to a stop in front of the Allerton Community Church and let the engine idle.

Tracy took a fast peek into the rearview mirror. "Do I look all right?" All she had to wear was the same skirt and blouse that she had worn to Keith's office.

"You look great."

"Right." Tracy made a face. She clambered down to the sidewalk. "Drive carefully and say hi to Paul for me." Maggie was taking the day off to attend church in Brockton where her brother was conducting the service.

"Mr. Perkins said he'd drive you home," Maggie reminded her. "You don't want to walk two miles in those heels."

"Thanks, Mother Hen." Mr. Perkins was an elderly gentleman who sometimes helped out at the kennels. Leave it to Maggie to make all the arrangements for her.

Maggie waved as the truck rumbled away from the curb. Tracy stood for a moment gazing up at the tall steeple. When she was young, she firmly believed that the spire reached all the way to heaven. The simple straight lines of the old building gave her a sense of peace.

Palm Sunday. With all that had happened during the past few days, she almost forgot that

Holy Week was beginning.

She was nearly trampled as a gaggle of children burst out of the side door waving palm fronds. The children were followed by a frantic young woman who was trying to coax them into a line. She looked like a harried shepherd with an unruly flock of lambs. If Tracy didn't hurry inside, she would miss their grand processional.

She wasn't sure of her reception by the members. Three years ago, most of the congregation stood by her while Keith dropped sly hints and insinuations about her character, but there were a few who apparently wished she would find another church.

She needn't have worried. She was greeted warmly with hugs and handshakes. There were a few who didn't seem to see her, but she decided to give them the benefit of the doubt.

As she looked for a place to sit, she spotted Keith and his wife in the second row "Bradford pew." If she was lucky, he wouldn't notice her. She wanted to hear the judge's decision about the temporary conservator and the guardian ad litem, but church wasn't the place to discuss business.

Quietly she slipped into a pew and sat back, enjoying the familiar scene. Several of the choir members were waving hello, and she waggled her fingers at them. Rev. Edwards—or Rev. Jim, as everyone called him—smiled at her from the pulpit. Some of the older members still referred to him as the new minister. He had only been with the church for six years.

And then she recognized Leif Ericson sitting in the bass section of the choir. That shouldn't be too much of a surprise. His deep voice probably reached the lowest note ever written.

The processional music began, and the children paraded in. Triumphantly waving their palm fronds, they managed to muss some hairdos among the ladies sitting along the aisle, but no one seemed to mind

The service was joyful, the music was inspiring, and Rev. Jim's sermon really touched her heart. During the sermon he spoke of Jesus' healing as he traveled the road to Jerusalem. She prayed that the Lord's healing power would touch her brother.

After the benediction, she joined the line waiting to shake the minister's hand. Although several people hurried past her without a word, a crowd gathered around her, welcoming her back and asking about Jeff. She felt wrapped in love.

By the time she reached the door, she found Leif trailing behind her. There was no escaping the chief of police. She had seen him in jeans and a windbreaker, she had seen him in uniform, and now she added a suit and tie to the list. It pained her to admit that he looked good in any of them.

A very attractive young woman clung to his arm, gazing adoringly into his eyes. She looked like a Shirley Temple doll with blond ringlets framing her heart-shaped face, bedecked in a glittering array of gold—earrings, necklace, bracelets, rings. This had to be Mrs. Leif. Somehow, this woman wasn't the type Tracy imagined Leif would choose as his wife—not that she spent a lot of time thinking about him.

Rev. Jim took her hand and then gave her a hug. "Tracy, it's great to have you here. I heard your beautiful voice when we sang the hymns. We'd love to have you join the choir again."

She fumbled for a response. "I—I'm not sure how long I'll be in town. It all depends on Jeff's condition."

"I understand," he said gently. "Leif tells me he's in critical condition. We're all praying for him."

She fought back the tears that were welling. "Thank you. He needs everyone's prayers."

Tracy couldn't help but notice the long look the pastor exchanged with Leif. Was there something about Jeff they weren't telling her?

Rev. Jim continued, "Just remember that we love you. Even if you're only here for a few weeks, we hope you'll join us."

"The whole choir was talking about you," Leif added. "They'd really like to have you come back."

Tracy tensed. She was being backed into a corner. When she returned to Allerton, she had no intention of getting involved with the townspeople again—particularly with the police chief. "I'll—I'll think about it," she mumbled.

"I hope to go in and visit Jeff this week, and we'll pray for you too," Rev. Jim assured her.

"Thanks. I need that." Tracy shook the minister's hand again and then hurried outside. She didn't want any more pressure to join the choir, and she didn't want to miss her ride home. But there was no sign of Mr. Perkins. She looked uneasily around the parking lot. Mr. Perkins was a dear old man, but a bit forgetful.

Most of the congregation had already departed. Could she possibly walk home barefoot? She'd never make it in her heels.

And then Leif's SUV came to a stop in front of her. "Need a ride?" he boomed.

"Mr. Perkins will take me home," she called back.

Leif surveyed the parking lot. "I don't think so, Tracy. His car is gone. Hop in."

Tracy glanced over her shoulder. Keith and Louise Bradford were saying goodbye to Rev. Jim. She needed to make a fast decision—accept Leif's invitation or tangle with Keith again. No contest. She hurried to scramble into the SUV.

The front passenger seat was empty. Where was Mrs. Leif? Instead, she found two young boys sitting in the back, sporting Red Sox baseball caps. Miniature versions of Leif, they both eyed her curiously.

Blessings came in small packages. The boys would serve as a diversion from Leif's endless questions. He already knew more about her than her own mother. "This must be Mark and Luke," she said brightly.

"Right," Leif confirmed. "Mark is ten and Luke is seven. Say hello to Miss Dixon, guys."

"Hello, Miss Dixon," they chorused shyly.

Tracy had to smile at their solemn faces. "And you're both baseball players?"

The boys nodded in tandem.

"Future Red Sox stars," Leif announced proudly.

"Great," Tracy cheered. "I'm a diehard Red Sox fan." She decided she wouldn't give Leif time for another cross-examination today. She turned back to the boys. "What position do you play, Mark?"

"Mostly left field," Mark answered. "Sometimes coach lets me pitch."

"And how about you, Luke?"

"Mostly I sit on the bench," Luke confessed.

Tracy smothered a smile. The boys were adorable.

In minutes Leif turned into Tracy's driveway. She put a staying hand on his arm. "Wait just one more minute. I have something the boys might like to have."

Leif turned off the engine. "Take your time."

Tracy hurried upstairs to her room. Rifling through a box of souvenirs, she found it—a baseball. She'd wanted to get rid of that baseball for years—it brought too many memories of Keith—but she never had the heart to throw it away.

She rushed back down to the car. "Boys," she announced, "a friend of mine caught this ball at Fenway Park. Manny Ramirez fouled it into the stands where we were sitting. Would you like to have it?"

Two jaws dropped simultaneously. "Manny Ramirez," breathed Mark.

"Manny Ramirez," echoed Luke.

Mark reverently put out his hand to accept the gift. His eyes were wider than home plate. "Thank you, Miss Dixon," he whispered.

"Thank you, Miss Dixon," echoed Luke.

Leif chuckled. "You know you've just made two friends for life."

Tracy tried not to notice the way his eyes twinkled when he smiled. "That sounds good. I need all the friends I can get."

Mark seemed so shy she was surprised when he spoke up. "I have a baseball game Friday. Maybe you could come."

"Mark," Leif cautioned, "Miss Dixon is a busy lady."

Tracy suspected Leif was trying to shield his boys from contamination by the queen of crime, but she was touched by Mark's invitation. "I'd love to come. I haven't been to a baseball game in ages."

"It starts at three o'clock," Mark explained, "at the field behind the high school."

"I'll be there," Tracy promised. "I wouldn't miss it." She turned back to Leif. "Thanks so much for the ride. It would have been a long walk."

"No problem. I can get away Tuesday if you want to go into Boston to see Jeff again."

Tracy was torn. The more she tried to avoid Leif, the more she became involved with him. But she did want to see Jeff. Maybe there would be some small sign of improvement—some ray of hope. She gave in. "If it's not too much of an imposition, I would like to go."

"Pick you up at nine." Leif gave her a salute and put the SUV in reverse.

Leif didn't crack a smile, but there were two grinning young faces in the window as they rolled away. She gave the boys two thumbs up.

****

Tracy climbed into the passenger seat of Leif's

SUV. It was beginning to feel like her second home. She spent more time here than in her own house. But she felt a little uncomfortable, as though she were under surveillance. Leif seemed to be watching and waiting for her to make a misstep.

He threw her a brief nod as he set the car in motion. "Another nice day. No April showers."

"I'm ready for May flowers," Tracy countered. Summer couldn't come soon enough. She had bundled up for the cool weather in a yellow sweater and navy pants. Leif was not in uniform today. He wore jeans and a red sweatshirt with "Boston University" emblazoned across the front in bold white letters.

She decided on her strategy for today. Instead of letting Leif pump her for information, she would ask the questions. A good offense was the best defense.

His sweatshirt gave her the opening she needed. "Did you go to B.U.?"

Leif nodded. "Criminal justice major."

"I guess red and white are the school colors."

"Scarlet and white," he corrected her.

Tracy frowned. "Is there a difference?"

Leif pretended to look shocked. "B.U.'s mascot is a Boston Terrier. Why do you think they named him Rhett?"

"No guess," Tracy admitted.

"Because no one loves Scarlet more than Rhett." He managed to keep a straight face.

She had to laugh. "You win." So, the great stone face had a sense of humor. She debated her next question. She had never pried into a man's personal life, but he seemed a little more approachable today. "What brought you to Allerton?"

"It's a long story."

He hesitated. Tracy was afraid he was going to leave it at that, but he went on.

"My brother moved here last year while I was with the Boston P.D. Six months ago Val's plane went down in a thunderstorm. He and his wife Anne were both badly smashed up—fractured skulls, multiple broken bones, internal injuries." He paused again as he jockeyed the SUV onto the Interstate.

"Someone had to take care of the boys. I was planning to bring them into Boston to live with me when I found out Allerton was looking for a police chief."

"So Mark and Luke are your nephews?" Tracy felt an unexpected lift in her spirits.

He nodded. "But I couldn't love them more if they were my own."

Tracy understood that. The boys were so precious. She shivered, thinking of their ordeal. "That must have been a terrible time for them—for the whole family. Are Val and Anne all right now?"

Leif's face darkened. "Not one-hundred percent. Eventually they're both expected to make a full recovery, but it's going to take some time."

Since the day she looked into the muzzle of his Smith and Wesson, Tracy had tried to dislike Leif Ericson. But what do you do about a man who had totally turned his life upside down to take care of his family?

She studied the sharp planes of his face. He was usually so close-mouthed. When he wasn't asking questions, he communicated in three or four word sound bites. But today he had opened up. Maybe there was some hope that he considered her more than just another felon?

"Don't you miss Boston? Allerton must seem pretty dull compared to the big city."

Leif actually smiled. "It was quite a change. But I like the laid-back atmosphere here. And I do have some interesting cases." He threw her a knowing look.

Tracy felt her cheeks reddening. The conversation was getting a little too personal. She hurried on to the next question on her list. "Was that your wife in church with you Sunday?"

Leif took his eyes off the road long enough to throw her a confused frown. "I'm not married. Are you talking about Sheila Dunn? She's just another member of the choir."

"Oh," Tracy said meekly. She had noticed that Leif didn't wear a wedding ring, but that didn't prove anything. And no matter what he thought about the lady in question, Sheila Dunn clearly believed that she was a lot more to him than just another member of the choir.

But Leif's social life was not her business. Married or not, he was still just one step away from throwing her in jail.

They were nearing the outskirts of Boston. She wanted to ask Leif about his friendship with Jeff, but she subsided into silence as she tried to prepare herself for the emotional impact of seeing her brother again. At least she had some idea what to expect this time. And she was not going to soak Leif's sweatshirt with her tears today.

****

They stood side by side, peering through the glass wall at the motionless figure. It was still almost impossible to see Jeff's features; his face was still grossly swollen. The tightness in her chest almost cut off her breath. *You are not going to cry*, she told herself.

She focused on the screens around his bed, trying to read his vital signs, but the numbers were just a blur. She barely noticed when the doctor joined them.

"Miss Dixon, the nurse told me you were here."

"Dr. Burrows." Everything in her screamed, *Please give us some hope*, but she managed to keep her emotions in check. "Thank you for seeing us. We're anxious for an update on Jeff."

Her heart nearly stopped when the doctor hesitated. "Miss Dixon, I don't want to give you false hope. Jeff's chances are still less than fifty-fifty. Everything is strictly day-to-day. In any event, he'll feel worse before he feels better. So far the skin grafts seem to be going well, but it will be some time before we know if they have adhered successfully."

She couldn't speak, but she nodded.

The doctor patted her shoulder, trying to offer some comfort. "I will call you if there is any unexpected change in his condition."

She managed to choke out her thanks. As the doctor left them, she turned to look at Leif. Police officers dealt with injuries and death every day. They learned to stifle their emotions, but his pain was visible - his whole body tense, his fists clenched at his side. His badge and his gun were useless here. He had no weapons to help Jeff.

"Leif," she whispered. "Would you say a prayer for him?"

He nodded. They faced each other, bowing their heads as they clasped hands.

He began haltingly. "Father, God, we are asking today for your shield of protection around our brother in Christ. He was lost, but he was finding his way back to you. Bring him through this valley of the shadow and return him to us, strong and well. Amen."

"Amen," she responded. She remained standing with her head bowed, when an overwhelming sense of peace began to flow through her. Somehow she felt God's presence promising her that all would be well with Jeff.

That blessed assurance left her speechless, but it buoyed her spirits as they returned to the parking lot. And then she realized she was clinging to Leif's arm. She pulled away quickly. She couldn't rely on this man she hardly knew—especially while she was the object of a police investigation.

Besides, Leif had enough problems of his own. And he had every reason to mistrust her. He knew about her part in the theft of Ronda Starr's jewelry, and by now he had probably heard all the rumors about her shady past in Allerton. And yet, she felt something happening between them—a closeness that was almost scary.

They were on the ramp to the interstate before she found her voice. "Thanks for your prayer, Leif. It really lifted me up."

"Did you feel it?" he asked. "That God was saying yes."

"God's answer seemed so clear," she breathed. "I never felt anything that strongly before."

"Now I know what it means—the peace that passeth all understanding."

Shaken by the power of that peace, she was grateful when they drove on in silence. But she remembered the final question she needed to ask him. "Leif, tell me about your friendship with Jeff? How did you meet him? How did you earn his trust?"

He looked uncomfortable. "Actually, Tracy, I first ran into him when I had to pick him up for public intoxication. He passed out on the sidewalk in front of the drug store."

"Oh, no." Thinking of Jeff's humiliation was unbearable.

"I could have put him in the drunk tank, but I decided to take him home instead. By the time I got him under the shower and poured some coffee into him, he was fairly coherent. We sat and talked for a long time. He really opened up about his injuries and his depression."

"That's hard to believe." She had never been able to penetrate the stonewall Jeff had erected. Leif must have worked some kind of magic. "Jeff would never discuss his problems with anyone."

"I know. Maybe he was just grateful that I didn't arrest him. Anyway, I fell into the habit of stopping by the house occasionally. We'd sit and chew the fat about anything and everything. I told him how Jesus helped my brother and his wife through their injuries, but I tried not to be preachy. And then one day he asked to go to church with me. I think he was getting tired of living like a lost soul."

So Leif helped to pull her brother out of the pit. It was a comfort to know that Jeff had begun to make peace with the Lord.

"I can't find words to thank you enough. If only Jeff can make it through this."

They were approaching the exit for Allerton, when Leif spoke again. "Did Henry tell you he tracked down an engine for your car? He figures he should have it ready to go in about a week."

Tracy could have done cartwheels down the exit ramp. "Thank goodness. That's the best news I've had in ages." It would be a blessing to have wheels again.

Of course, now she had to figure out how to pay for the repairs. A credit card might help, but the debt still had to be paid. She made the decision to stay in Allerton. Jeff would need help when he was released from the hospital. When, she emphasized, not if. With a car she could get a job, maybe wait tables at Fisherman's Landing again. They always needed waitresses, and tourist season was coming soon.

She would have to make some plans, but they were pulling into her driveway. "Leif, you have been a godsend. When I have my car, I can quit bothering you."

His stern features softened. "You know it's not a bother. Jeff is my brother too."

She took a last glance at his rugged face as she climbed down from the SUV. Was it gratitude she felt for Leif or was it becoming something more? She had to fight the attraction. She was the sinner. He was the law. She was asking for heartbreak if she let herself fall for him.

Having her own car again would help to break

the connection between them. She had to end their relationship before she was in too deep.

Leif waited until she unlocked the front door and then backed the SUV out of the driveway. She pulled the door open and stopped, paralyzed. What had happened? The living room had been ransacked. Seat cushions were torn out. Books were thrown aside. Desk drawers hung open. Papers littered the floor. Even the piano bench had been emptied of sheet music.

Tracy backed out the door. She had to catch Leif. Rushing down the driveway, she shouted his name. But her heart sank. He was already several hundred feet down the road. She plunged into the street, waving her arms and shouting his name. Could he see her? The SUV wasn't slowing down.

CHAPTER VI

Tracy sagged in relief as the SUV made a sharp U-turn and raced back toward her. *Thank you, Lord.* In spite of all her good resolutions, she had to depend on Leif again. There was nowhere else to turn.

He jammed on his brakes and hit the ground running. "What's happened?" he shouted. "What's wrong?"

She forced herself to form the words. "Someone—someone has torn the house apart."

Leif charged past her up the driveway and came to a stop in the open door. "Have you touched anything?"

She crept up behind him, trying to peer around his wide shoulders. "I think just the doorknob." At this point she wasn't sure of anything.

Numb, she watched Leif pull out his radio. "Lucille, send Will out here fast. We've got a break-in at the Dixons." He turned to her. "Are you all right?"

She nodded wordlessly. She couldn't speak the words that were in her head, *As long as you're here.* She lifted her chin and put on her brave face.

"I want you to go sit in the SUV while I search the house. The burglar may still be inside." He shifted into police officer mode.

Tracy hadn't even considered that possibility. It didn't help her raw nerves to realize that a criminal might be holed up somewhere in the house. She wanted to follow Leif, but she knew she would only interfere with his investigation. Slowly she trudged to his car and sank into the seat, dropping her head into her hands.

It seemed like hours until he came back, but the scattered remnants of her common sense told her it was less than ten minutes. He came to the car window, his eyes full of compassion. "The burglar forced the lock on the back door. Just hang on a little longer, Tracy. I need to get my fingerprint kit."

The numbness began to wear off. As he retrieved his equipment, she saw a patrol car come to a stop in front of the house. She recognized the police sergeant who climbed out. Will Robbins was an old high school classmate. Wearily she watched as the two men conferred and then came back to her window.

Will wore a sheepish look. "I'm sorry about this," he apologized, as though the whole mess were his fault. "Are you OK?"

"Just a little wobbly," she admitted. Now that was the understatement of the year. She trembled all over in an effort to hold herself together. She had no patience with women who fell apart when the going got tough, but this break-in was the shove that pushed her over the edge. The worst part was the feeling of violation, picturing a stranger in her home, pawing through her clothing and her personal possessions.

"Tracy, dusting for prints is messy," Leif explained. "If this crook had any brains, he wore gloves, so Will is just going to dust in a few of the most likely spots. But I need to ask you a few questions."

She nodded. Her voice had deserted her.

Leif swung into his seat behind the steering wheel and pulled out a notebook. "Tell me what valuables you keep in the house?"

She was struck by a bolt of panic. Her money. Did the burglar find her money? "I had three hundred dollars in cash in a dresser drawer."

What would she do if her money was gone? That was the last of her severance pay from Mr. Rifkin. It was all she had to live on until she found work. "That's about all," she whispered. "I don't own anything really valuable."

Leif kept digging. "What about Jeff? Did he have anything of value?"

If only her brain would stop misfiring and let her concentrate. She shook her head. "You know Jeff. He didn't care about things. I don't think he had anything that would interest a thief."

He took both her hands in his. His touch calmed her and gave her courage.

"Tracy, I'm going to check to see if your money is gone. We need to find out if this guy was looking for cash or for something else. Tell me where you kept the money."

"It was in an envelope with a letter in the top drawer of my dresser. It wasn't really hidden." How could she have been so careless? Allerton seemed so safe, so far removed from big city crime.

"I'll be right back." He stepped down from the car and disappeared into the house. Tracy realized her privacy was totally doomed. Now it would be Leif prowling through her personal life.

He returned in minutes. "The cash is still there. Your burglar was looking for something else."

Tracy didn't realize she had been holding her breath until she released it in a huge sigh of relief. No matter what else the burglar stole, her money was safe. She didn't have to give up eating.

But Leif wasn't finished. "Now, I need you to think hard—not just about money. Is there anything else in the house that someone would want—antiques, art work, a collection of any kind, like coins or stamps, or even medications?"

"I just don't know," she confessed. The Dixons were more into flea markets and garage sales than antique shops and art auctions.

"OK. I know you're upset, but keep trying to think of something—anything. I'm going to see how Will is doing. Just try to relax."

A sensation of loneliness overwhelmed her as Leif disappeared again. Tilting the seat back, she closed her eyes. It might make her feel better to cry, but she didn't have enough energy for that.

Another half hour passed before the men finished their work and Leif waved her into the house. She was so exhausted she could have dropped onto the old plaid sofa and slept for a month—if the cushions hadn't been scattered all over the living room floor.

"We've picked up a few prints," he explained, "but they may be yours or Jeff's. Are your fingerprints on file anywhere?"

Tracy remembered that humiliating moment in New York when Detective Diaz took her prints. She felt like Public Enemy Number One. "With the New York police," she admitted.

"I'm going to stay here and help clean up the mess while Will takes the evidence to the station." Leif turned to his officer. "Will, after you get things squared away at the station, I want you to pick up a couple of deadbolts and some door chains from the hardware store."

"Got you, Chief." Will gave them a salute and hurried off to the patrol car.

Leif's face was grim when he turned back to her. "Tracy, while we're cleaning up this mess, I want you to identify anything that's missing. This guy was looking for something specific."

She nodded, hoping her brain would start functioning.

Restoring order to the chaos was a monumental task. The thief had done a thorough job of trashing the whole house. She would have given up if it were not for Leif's endless patience. While she put sofa cushions and drawers back in place, he cleaned up the residue of the fingerprint dust.

They worked side by side, going room to room. As far as she could tell, nothing was missing. The only thing that suffered serious damage was her sense of security. She had never been a timid soul, but suddenly the world was a scary place.

When Will returned, the two men went back to work, installing dead bolts and chains on the front and back doors. Tracy trailed along behind them as they toured the whole house, checking the latches on the windows. If the thief came back, he would have to work a lot harder and smarter to find a way in.

It took hours before everything was restored to what passed for normal. Tracy didn't object when Leif ordered her into the recliner. She needed to sit down before she fell down. He eyed her with a worried frown. "Will you be afraid to stay here alone tonight? Maybe you should stay with friends."

She knew he was right. There was no way she would sleep in this house tonight. "I'll call Maggie," she conceded.

She dreaded the moment Leif would leave, but he was gathering up his equipment. She managed to push herself to her feet. "Leif, I know you're tired of hearing me say this, but thank you, thank you, thank you."

He gazed down at her for a long moment. Although his craggy features revealed no emotion, there was a deep intensity in those sea-gray eyes. He looked as though he intended to wrap her in his arms and kiss her senseless. She held her breath, knowing she wouldn't resist. The silence stretched between them like a taut wire.

And then he broke the silence. "Promise me you'll go to Maggie's," he said, turning toward the door.

****

Maggie waited in her battered pickup truck as Tracy came across the parking lot at Fisherman's Landing, the seafood restaurant. "How'd you make out?" Maggie called.

Tracy gave her a grin and two thumbs up. "I start Sunday."

Maggie pumped her fist in a victory celebration.

"I'll just be working weekends for now," Tracy bubbled as she climbed into the cab. "But that should be enough to keep me alive. There's a new manager, but LeBlanc is still the maitre d', and I remember several of the waitresses."

Maggie wheeled the truck out onto the highway. "Will you need a ride to work?"

"Just this Sunday, I hope. Henry says my car should be ready Wednesday or Thursday."

"Do you think Leif would be available to take you to work? Bud and I are going to his Mom's for Easter dinner. I can take you home afterwards."

"Don't worry about it. I'll find a ride." Tracy hoped she wouldn't have to bother Leif again. "It will be so great to have wheels. I hate asking people to cart me around."

"I don't mind taking a break from the kennels," Maggie insisted. "Working with dogs all day, I begin to forget what people look like."

Tracy laughed. "Maggie, you've been a gem. Thanks for giving me refuge last night. I know I would have thrashed around in bed all night alone at my house."

Maggie threw her a concerned glance. "Are you sure you want to go home? You know you're welcome to stay with us as long as you want."

Tracy hesitated. She suspected she would never feel safe in her own home again, but unless she made a permanent move to Maggie's, she needed to deal with her fear. She put on an air of confidence she didn't feel. "I'll be all right. Whoever broke in knows that there's nothing there worth stealing. And Leif and Will put deadbolts and chains on the doors."

"You need a dog. A big dog that eats burglars in one gulp."

"Right." Tracy groaned. "A big dog that eats forty tons of chow a day. I'd better wait until I can afford a few groceries."

"I'd still feel better if you owned a dog."

"What I need is a financial advisor." Tracy's brain rang up dollars like a cash register. "I have to send rent money to my roommate in New York and tell her to find someone else to share the apartment. And then I need to send her more money so she can ship me my things. I've been rotating the same three outfits for almost two weeks. And then I've got to pay Henry for the repairs on the car. And then ..."

"OK, OK." Maggie conceded defeat. "Maybe a Chihuahua."

"Oh, sure!" Tracy gave Maggie's arm a light punch. "He could nibble the burglar into submission."

But Maggie veered off in another direction. "If you're working on Sunday, will you have to miss the Easter service?"

"No, my hours work out perfectly. I don't have to go in until four on Sunday afternoons. But I do have one favor to ask. I'd like to use your computer occasionally to check their website. They post information about special events."

"I take it you never figured out the password to your brother's computer."

Tracy made a face. "No, I gave up trying. I only used my roommate's computer for my homework and to e-mail you or Jeff. I don't miss wading through all that spam."

As they approached her house, Tracy spotted a flashy black sports car parked in her driveway. "Do you know any burglars who drive a Maserati?"

"Sure," Maggie snapped. "The crook who drives that car is none other than Keith Allen Bradford."

"Keith!" She didn't need to fight off Keith's attentions today.

"Do you want me to come in with you?"

"That's OK. I can deal with him." Tracy didn't want to drag Maggie into any more of her problems, but she wasn't looking forward to this visit.

As Maggie brought the truck to a stop, Tracy gathered up her purse and her overnight bag. "Thanks so much for everything, Maggie. I owe you at least two days work at the kennels."

Maggie leaned over to kiss her cheek. "You better watch out. I might take you up on that."

Tracy waved as Maggie whirled away with a blast of her horn. She turned to find Keith getting out of his car to greet her. Had his smile always looked that artificial? She must have been hopelessly naïve to imagine herself in love with such a selfish, self-centered egotist.

"So here you are! I was just about to give up on you." Keith threw an arm around her shoulders, but Tracy turned her head quickly so that his kiss landed in her hair. He refused to get the message that his attentions were not welcome.

"What brings you here, Keith?" She managed to keep the irritation out of her voice.

"The judge has appointed me temporary conservator of Jeff's assets. I need to review his financial situation." He gave her a self-satisfied smirk. He actually expected her to be thrilled by the news.

"You could have called and asked me to come into your office," she reminded him.

"I thought your home would be a friendlier atmosphere." That suggestive tone was back in his voice.

As she unlocked the door, Tracy tried to swallow her anger. Somehow she had known that the judge would choose Keith for this job. She hoped they could take care of Jeff's business in one brief meeting.

"We'd better sit in the kitchen. I've tried to gather up everything you'll need."

Keith ignored her suggestion and settled himself on the living room sofa. "This will be fine right here."

Tracy remained standing. The man was pure brass—making himself completely at home. But she wasn't his innocent bedazzled little fiancée anymore. She could hold her own. "Do you know who's been appointed guardian-ad-litem?"

Keith hesitated, surprised at her icy tone. "Yes, you may have heard of him. John Whitby. He's a retired judge."

"And he'll be investigating me?"

Keith nodded. "He's a bit stuffy, but he'll be fair. You can expect a visit from him any day now."

She swallowed hard. A judge. That didn't give her much hope that she would be appointed Jeff's conservator. Retrieving Jeff's papers from the desk, she tried to hand them to Keith, but instead of taking the papers, he patted the spot beside himself on the sofa.

Gritting her teeth, she sat down. The sofa was so worn, the springs sagged and tilted her against him. Instantly, as though she had been scalded, she jerked upright and pulled away from him.

She fought to bury her disgust under an all-business manner. "Jeff's disability check is direct-deposited at the bank. His utility bills are paid by automatic debit to that account. I think the tax bill is the only problem."

Like Jekyll and Hyde, Keith transformed into his professional attorney mode. Carefully he checked through the assortment of bills and bank statements. "I'll go to the bank tomorrow and get a cashier's check to take care of the tax bill. What else do we need to deal with?"

Tracy frowned. "I think that's all for now."

"What about his automobile insurance? Has anyone reported his accident to the insurance company? Do you know where the car is? I understand it was totally destroyed."

She was caught unprepared. "I never thought about the car," she admitted. "The state police should know where it is. And I should be able to find out about Jeff's auto insurance." She started to struggle to her feet. "I'll see if I can find the policy."

She lost her balance as Keith grasped her arm. Playfully he pulled her down into his lap. "The insurance can wait. I can think of other things I'd rather do right now."

She tried to pull away as he nuzzled her neck. Trembling with fury she braced her hands against his chest and shoved with all her strength. Keith laughed as though her resistance was just part of a game.

A loud knock at the door froze them both in place. Instantly he released her. Free from his grasp, she surged to her feet. "Who is it?"

That blessed rumble answered. "It's Leif, picking you up for choir practice."

Thank you, Lord. If Leif had come to arrest her, she would have been happy to go off to jail with him. She never intended to join the choir. She had even forgotten that tonight was rehearsal night. But suddenly she couldn't imagine any place she would rather be than at choir practice.

Bursting with gratitude, she threw open the door. "Come in, Leif. I'll be ready in a minute. We're finished with our business here." She threw a meaningful look at Keith. "As soon as I find the auto insurance policy, I'll bring it to you—at the office," she stated plainly.

Keith resumed his urbane charm. "That will be fine." He tucked in his shirt, straightened his tie, and smoothed his hair as he nodded to Leif. "It's nice to see you again, Chief." With the papers under his arm, he strolled nonchalantly to the door.

"Have a good evening, Mr. Bradford." Leif measured every step Keith took as he left the house. It gave Tracy a huge sense of satisfaction to see the scowl on the Viking's face.

****

Tracy felt a wave of nostalgia as she took her place with the other sopranos in the choir room. She started singing with the cherub choir when she was three years old. She couldn't remember missing a rehearsal in all the years that followed—with the junior choir, the teen choir, the senior choir—until she left Allerton.

Old Mrs. Edson was still the director and prim Miss Templeton was still the accompanist, as though her three years in New York never happened.

She waved to Maggie among the altos. Maggie stared at her in disbelief. "You came!" she mouthed.

Tracy shrugged with a helpless lift of her hands.

She tucked her feet under her chair, making room for Miss Shirley Temple, Sheila Dunn, to edge her way to the seat beside her. Immediately Tracy sensed an air of hostility. Leif said the choir wanted her back, but apparently that had not been a unanimous ballot. Sheila's vote would have been a definite, "No way. Absolutely not."

Sheila turned to her with a lofty air. "I didn't expect to see you here. You didn't sound too enthusiastic about joining us."

"Leif sort of kidnapped me." Tracy forced a smile. "But I'm glad I came."

Icicles dripped from Sheila's voice. "Well, don't think that makes you special," she sniffed. "Leif is always helping somebody."

Tracy didn't bother to respond. She took a quick glance over her shoulder at Leif in the bass section. He was leafing through his music folder, totally unaware of the frigid temperature two rows ahead of him. So if Leif didn't think she was special, what did he think of her?

CHAPTER VII

The aluminum bleachers were crammed with excited parents, grandparents, brothers, sisters, and townspeople. When the crowd stamped their feet to pump up the team, Tracy actually felt herself bounce off her seat. The major leagues weren't able to compete with Allerton Little League when it came to crowd support.

It was fun to be out in the fresh air, thinking about something other than her problems. Maybe Leif didn't want her here, but he was stuck with her. She really did love baseball, and she refused to disappoint Mark. With Leif on one side of her and Luke on the other, she felt like a member of the cheerleading squad. They stood in unison to shout encouragement as Mark stepped up to the plate. His shirt proclaimed that his team, the Spark Plugs, was sponsored by Henry's Garage.

Henry's Spark Plugs were down a run with two outs, but they had runners on first and second base. Tracy could see why Leif was convinced that Mark would play for the Red Sox some day. Patrolling left field, he made some spectacular catches, and his teammates looked to him for leadership. For a boy who was so quiet and shy off the field, he exuded skill and confidence on the diamond.

They groaned like a Greek chorus as Mark took a called strike. "Better have your eyes checked, Ump," complained one partisan fan.

The next two pitches were balls. The tension mounted. The count reached three balls and two strikes. Tracy realized she was clutching Leif's arm. She pried her fingers loose as the pitcher went into his wind-up.

Thwack. Mark's swing sent the ball into orbit, soaring over the heads of the outfielders and the chain link fence at the end of the playground. The two runners dashed toward home plate while Mark trotted easily around the bases. The Spark Plugs were up six to four and the team whooped with joy.

"Way to go, Mark!" Tracy was jumping up and down. "You're the best!" Her voice rang out over all the commotion.

People turned their heads to stare at her. Blushing, she forced herself to sit down and close her mouth. Leif smothered a smile, pretending he had no idea who she was.

The next batter tried to outdo Mark. He took a wild swing at the first pitch. The ball popped high in the air and then plummeted down toward the bleachers.

Determined to catch the foul ball, Luke scrambled to his feet and climbed up onto his seat. With all his attention focused on the ball, he edged further and further along the bench.

Tracy leaped to her feet. "Luke, watch out," she shouted. "You're getting too close to the end."

But her warning came too late. Blindly, with arms outstretched, Luke cartwheeled over the railing at the end of the bleachers.

"Luke!" Leif yelled. Jumping over two rows of seats at a time, he hit the ground before Tracy reacted. "Please, Lord," she gasped, scrambling after Leif, squeezing through the crowd.

Her heart came to a stop as she rounded the corner. Luke lay on his back, stunned and silent. Blood gushed from a deep gash on his arm. His eyes were open, but he stared off into space.

Leif kneeled at Luke's side and pressed a handkerchief against the wound. But it did nothing to staunch the bleeding. An anxious crowd gathered around them.

"Tracy." Leif's voice was taut. "Come with me. Dr. Wilson is out of town. I'll have to take Luke to the emergency room in Plymouth. Ellie," he shouted to his neighbor, "take care of Mark."

Leif swept Luke up in his arms and raced toward the SUV. Tracy ran after them. She leaped into the passenger seat as Leif opened the door. He thrust Luke into her arms. "Keep pressure on the wound," he urged.

The handkerchief was already drenched with blood. Leif paused long enough to throw her a clean towel from the back of the truck. He slapped the bubble light onto the roof and they roared out onto the road with lights flashing.

Luke lay limp and lifeless in her arms. "Luke, are you all right?" she whispered. "Talk to me." If only he would say something – make a sound.

He looked up at her with saucer eyes. With his face chalk white, he bit his lip trying to be brave, while his tears soaked into her shirt.

"It's OK honey. It'll be OK." She cuddled him closer to her heart, whispering a prayer as she put as much pressure as she dared on his arm.

"Hang on, big fellow." Leif encouraged. "We'll be there in a few minutes."

Luke finally gave in to his fears. "Do I gotta get a shot?" he sobbed.

Tracy pressed a kiss against his forehead. She didn't want to tell him a lie. "The doctor will fix you up good as new."

The eight miles to Jordan Hospital in Plymouth seemed like eighty. Her pulse raced faster than the truck as they barreled down Route 44. Luckily there weren't many cars on the road.

How much blood had the little guy lost? Was the

flow slowing at all? Tracy clutched Luke tight as they screeched to a halt at the entrance to the emergency room. Leif cut the engine and leaped out. Racing around the car, he snatched the boy out of her arms. Tracy sent up another fervent prayer as Leif carried him through the automatic doors.

Removing the keys, she jumped out of the car and hurried into the emergency room. Thank goodness, an orderly was already whisking Luke down the hall. Leif stood at the front desk, impatiently filling out the paperwork. "I'm his uncle." He was almost shouting. "I'll sign any authorization you need. Just take care of that boy."

His face tense, his jaw set, he turned away from the desk. He needed comfort as much as Luke did. And then he noticed her standing there. "Tracy," he groaned, "I'm sorry. Your clothes are ruined."

Tracy looked down at her shirt. She hadn't realized that her blouse was soaked with splotches of blood. But that was the least of her worries. "It doesn't matter," she insisted. "Luke matters."

"I'll get Mark's jacket from the car. It should fit you."

Tracy handed him the keys so he could move the SUV away from the entrance.

Leif looked relieved to have an outlet for his pent-up anxiety. "I'll be right back."

Three people sat in the waiting area, scanning listlessly through magazines or simply staring out the window. They all turned to gape at Tracy's bloodstained shirt.

Ignoring the stares, Tracy found a seat. Poor little Luke. What was happening? Had they stopped the bleeding? Was he still crying?

Leif returned with a nylon windbreaker. She pulled the jacket on over her blouse. The stains didn't bother her, but Luke would be frightened if he saw his own blood.

Leif dropped into the chair beside her, looking

whipped. He took her hand and they whispered a prayer together. History was repeating itself. Here they were again, side by side, anxiously waiting at a hospital for words of hope from a doctor. If only there was some way to reassure Leif. The calm, laid-back police chief was wound up tight. Once again he wasn't able to help.

And then they heard Luke's wails from the end of the hall. Leif leaped to his feet as a nurse hurried into the waiting area. She eyed the visitors. "Is there a Miss Dixon here?"

Tracy jumped up. "I'm here."

The nurse signaled Tracy to follow her. "Luke wants you to hold his hand while the doctor stitches him up."

"Of course!" Tracy hurried down the hall behind the nurse with Leif at her heels.

A white-coated young doctor was examining Luke's arm as they entered the cubicle. The boy's tear-stained face brightened at the sight of reinforcements. "I'm not a baby," he hiccupped.

"No," Leif assured him. "You're a big, strong boy."

"OK, big boy, you're going to be very brave and sit still for me," the doctor insisted.

Luke reached out a hand toward Tracy. She put an arm around him and pulled him close, resting his head against her shoulder. He seemed so small against the stark white hospital sheets.

She turned a worried eye toward Leif. He stood in the doorway, his strained face showing every inch of Luke's pain. The big tough cop was a marshmallow. Their gazes locked in a shared concern.

Luke stared at the needle in terror as the doctor prepared to stitch the wound. Was there a way to distract him?

She came up with a story. "Luke, I had a bad fall like yours when I was about your age."

Luke managed to drag his gaze away from the needle. "Wha—What happened?"

"Well, my brother and I had a tree house—way up high in a giant oak tree. It was so high we had to prop a ladder against the tree so we could climb up to the lowest branch. But guess what happened."

"What?" Luke's gaze was fixed on her. He didn't seem to be aware that the doctor was already putting stitches in his arm. Apparently they had given him a local anesthetic.

Tracy hurried on before she lost his attention. "We were playing a game in the tree house, and my brother was getting hungry. He started to climb down, but when he put his foot on the top rung of the ladder, he accidentally kicked it over. We were in really bad trouble. There was no way to get down from the tree."

"What did you do?"

"Well, we yelled and we shouted, but no one heard us. So we waited and waited and then we yelled some more. We were getting really hungry and it started to get dark, but no one came. We knew we would have to get ourselves down without any help."

"Wow!" Luke exclaimed.

"So my brother went first. He hung by his hands from the lowest branch for a while. It was like a hundred miles to the ground." Tracy stole a quick glance at Leif. He stood listening to her story with a half-smile, apparently as intrigued as his nephew.

"But he finally let go and bam—he dropped."

"Was he all right?" Luke worried.

"Jeff twisted his ankle, but he said he was OK. And then it was my turn. I was really scared."

After so many years, Tracy still remembered that feeling of panic. "I tried hanging by my hands like my brother, but I was afraid to let go. I just hung there and hung there. And, you know what? I'd still be hanging there right this minute, but my

71

hands were getting tired. They began to slip. And they slipped some more. And some more. And then— oops—I crashed to the ground like a ton of bricks."

"Were you hurt?"

"I had all the breath knocked out of me. It was spooky. All I could do was lie there, gasping for air. My brother was sure something awful had happened to me because I couldn't talk. He started to cry, but finally, I could breathe again. And then I discovered I wasn't even hurt. But you know what?"

"What?" Luke was wide-eyed.

"I never went up in that tree house again." Tracy gave Luke a huge smile as she finished her story. The doctor had completed his stitches and was already bandaging Luke's arm.

"Am I all done?" Luke asked in astonishment.

The doctor started giving instructions to Tracy, as though she were Luke's mother. "You'll need to come back next Friday or see your family doctor to have the stitches out," he began. Cheeks burning, she stepped back so Leif could get the information.

"Everything looks good, but watch for any sign of infection. Kids are hardy, but after a fall you should also keep an eye on him for any indication of internal bleeding or concussion."

Looking ten years younger, Leif shook the doctor's hand. "Thank you, doctor. We'll take good care of him." He swept Luke up into his arms again.

As they walked out to the SUV, Luke admired his bandage as though it were a medal of valor. "Wait till I show the guys," he bragged.

Although he had recovered from his trauma, Tracy settled the boy into her lap in the SUV. He'd be a hero in the schoolyard while his uncle recovered from a nervous breakdown. She kept her bloody blouse hidden under Mark's jacket. No need to traumatize the little Superboy. Hugging him close, she planted a kiss on top of his head.

She felt Leif's gaze as they backed out of their

parking space. There was a new glint in his eye—a gleam of gratitude instead of his usual look of suspicion or caution. And something more—a spark of intense heat.

She didn't want to guess what that spark meant, but it started a fire. The heat blazed through her as Leif spoke. "Thanks, Tracy. I don't know how you talked Luke through that. You are something special."

****

The whole family waited at the door as Leif carried Luke into the house. Although Luke's mother was still in a wheelchair with the injuries from the plane crash, Anne insisted on holding Luke in her lap. Val, his father, leaned on his crutches and hovered over them, while Mark danced circles around them.

Luke thoroughly enjoyed his role as the wounded hero. "I bleeded all over Miss Dixon," he said proudly. "And I didn't cry when the doctor stitched me up."

"Did you get the foul ball?" Mark asked as though Luke's injuries were secondary to something really important, like catching a baseball.

"Naw," Luke grumbled. "My shirt caught on the railing and I landed right on my catching arm."

"You were lucky you didn't break any bones, young man," his father put in.

"Or fracture your skull," his mother added.

"He must have inherited a thick head from the Ericson side of the family," Leif suggested.

"Did you win the game, Mark?" Luke steered the conversation back to the crucial matters.

"Yeah, we won by a mile. Once we got ahead, they couldn't catch us again. Coach gave me my home run ball to keep."

Luke squirmed out of his mother's arms. "I want to see it," he exclaimed.

With a whoop, the boys bounded out of the room

as though they were in a foot race. Looking after them, Anne sighed. "How come we didn't have a nice quiet little girl who just played with dolls all day?"

Val laughed. "With our luck we'd get a tomboy who spent all her time climbing trees."

Leif smiled, remembering Tracy's tale about her adventure with the tree house. She seemed to know just the right way to take Luke's mind off the doctor's stitching. He was trying to remain objective about Tracy's guilt or innocence, but today his suspicions lost ground to his gratitude and admiration. She had such tenderness in those gorgeous eyes as she cuddled Luke.

So far he had been fairly successful in resisting Tracy's beauty, but every time he was with her he found something new to attract him—her spunk, her compassion. The way she walked as though she were moving to music. The way she treated the boys as friends instead of pests.

"So Luke bled all over Miss Dixon," Val said. "Isn't she the one who was involved in the jewelry theft?"

"She's the one," Leif admitted. "Mark invited her to the game. I had to take her along to the hospital to keep pressure on Luke's wound while I drove."

Leif caught his brother's curious expression. Val and Anne were inveterate matchmakers. They tried to fix him up with every single woman in Massachusetts, from Cape Cod to the Berkshire Hills. They were way off base if they thought he was interested in Tracy Dixon. He knew the Lord would find the right woman for him, but in the meantime, he was a professional cop. It would be a mistake to get involved with a suspect. His only interest in Tracy was solving a crime.

And then an irritating voice in the back of his head caught his attention. *Just keep reminding yourself of that, Mr. Professional Cop.*

****

Tracy collapsed into the recliner in her living room, exhausted by the tension of the past few hours. She needed to change her clothes and soak her bloodstained shirt in cold water, but first she needed to just sit for a minute and get her second wind.

She groaned when she heard a knock at the door. Leif? No, he was taking Luke home to his parents. Don't let it be Keith again, she thought, struggling to her feet.

She didn't recognize the distinguished white-haired gentleman on her doorstep. "Miss Tracy Dixon?" he inquired. "I'm John Whitby."

Whitby! Tracy drew a long breath. The retired judge appointed as Jeff's guardian ad litem to investigate her. Wishing she could wave a wand and magically disappear, she realized what the judge was seeing—an exhausted woman with uncombed hair in wrinkled, bloodstained clothes.

"I'm Tracy Dixon," she managed. "Please come in."

"Is everything all right?" He stared uneasily at the splotches of blood. He probably thought she had just added murder to her rap sheet.

"Everything's fine now," she hurried to explain. "I just returned from the emergency room, helping a little boy with a gash on his arm."

The judge didn't look convinced, but he followed her into the living room and settled on the sofa. He spoke very formally as though this were a trial in his courtroom. "You have petitioned to be named conservator of your brother's assets. I believe you were notified that I have been appointed Jeffrey Dixon's guardian ad litem to investigate your qualifications to serve in that capacity."

"Yes, sir," Tracy mumbled. Her nerves were signaling a frantic SOS. She felt as though she were a defendant on trial.

"Are you and your brother close? Are you on

good terms?"

"Jeff and I are very close," she whispered. "We've been best friends since we were small."

"But you don't see each other often." The judge peered over his glasses like a scholarly owl.

"I live in New York—well, Brooklyn really." Explaining her aversion to visiting Allerton would make matters worse. Of course, Judge Whitby was probably well aware of her scandalous reputation in town.

"When was the last time you saw your brother before his accident?"

"I came home for a long weekend in October when my mother was getting ready to move to Florida."

"And you and your brother were on good terms then?"

Tracy swallowed hard. She hated to tell him that Jeff was drunk most of the time she was here. "We argued a little about his drinking," she admitted, "but I love Jeff dearly and he loves me."

"You have lived in New York how long?"

"Three years."

"And how often have you seen Jeffrey during that time?"

The judge must have been a prosecutor before his years on the bench. His questions went right to the heart of her relationship with her brother.

"He was in Iraq when I moved away. Then he was injured and they sent him to Walter Reid Hospital in Washington. I tried to visit him every weekend while he was there. Two years ago when he was released from the hospital, I came back here to help him get settled. And then the visit in October."

"So, you have seen him just once over the past two years."

Tracy muffled a groan. That sounded so cold, as though her family didn't count for much in her life. "But we talked by phone a lot and e-mailed several times a week."

The judge took a new tack. "What is your financial situation? Are you living on your savings now?"

Did the good judge think she wanted Jeff's money for herself? He obviously didn't have a very high opinion of her.

"No, I don't really have any money saved. The cost of living in New York is very high. I had a good job, but I wasn't able to put anything aside. I took classes at NYU. Most of my salary went for tuition and books. But I'm starting a new job Sunday at Fisherman's Landing."

The judge seemed to be mulling over her response. "I understand you are in trouble with the police in New York City."

She had been expecting that question since he walked in the door. Would the judge call Diaz? The detective would convince him that she was guilty. This was becoming a losing battle. "The police think I was involved in a theft, but that's not true. If they caught the real thief, I could prove my innocence."

"I believe you had another encounter with the law when you were in high school?"

Not that again. But she couldn't deny it. She couldn't tell a lie without blushing and stumbling over the knots in her tongue.

"I was accused of shoplifting, but honestly, Judge Whitby, I did not steal anything. I would never do that."

The judge didn't appear impressed. "I've heard some other rumors about your past."

She lifted her chin. "I don't know what you've been told, but there's nothing to those rumors." She wanted to explain why Keith had spread those lies about her shady past, but what good would that do? It was just her word against Keith's—the shoplifter vs. the state representative.

The judge sat there for a long moment,

apparently sizing her up. She looked him squarely in the eye, hoping he could read the truth.

"I think that's all for today," he announced, getting to his feet. "I'll be talking to a few people here in town. Thank you for meeting with me."

Tracy saw him to the door. As he walked to his car, a dismal thought settled over her like a heavy fog. She heaved a long sigh. "If I were the investigator, I wouldn't trust me either."

CHAPTER VIII

From his place in the choir loft, Leif looked out over the congregation. Easter - his favorite day of the year. Lilies covered every inch of space around the altar, and Tracy was singing his favorite Easter song, "The Holy City." Her silvery, sweet voice soared to the rafters of the old church. "Jerusalem, Jerusalem, lift up your voice and sing."

The glorious sound surged through him, raising goose bumps on his arms. He watched the rapt faces of the members, realizing that they were all touched by her too.

With the last note came a hushed silence and then a spontaneous outburst of applause. Tracy glowed as she went back to her seat with the other sopranos.

Leif spied Keith Bradford in his pew in the second row, brimming with self-importance as he joined in the applause. Irritation - or jealousy - gnawed at him as he remembered that Bradford had been at Tracy's house the evening he stopped by to pick her up for choir practice. Something about Bradford's cloying charm raised his hackles.

Tracy's cheeks were on fire when she came to the door that evening. She said something about an auto insurance policy, while Bradford fixed his tie and tucked in his shirt. That must have been quite a discussion they were having. Something was going on with those two.

Leif closed his eyes in a silent prayer. "Lord, I could use a little help here. I think I'm falling for this woman and I don't even trust her. There are too many arrows pointing in the wrong direction. Lord, you know I've been burned before. I let a woman make a fool of me, giving me the come-on while she set me up for her lover. I need to know the truth about Tracy. Is she as innocent as she seems or is she just another beautiful con artist?"

Leif couldn't erase the memory of Crystal's betrayal. His knee was a constant reminder that she had led him into a trap. He met Crystal Rivers while working undercover, gathering evidence to bring down drug kingpin, Chase Martinez.

Crystal came to the station house insisting she had information for the detective on the Martinez case. When they arranged to meet, Crystal told him her sister Mara was involved with Martinez, and she wanted to help bring him down. Crystal was an exotic beauty and an outrageous flirt, but he was dumb enough to be flattered by her obvious interest in him.

They began to meet regularly. Supposedly Crystal gleaned inside information about Martinez from her sister. Actually she fed him worthless bits of nothing. And then Crystal told him her sister was missing. She invited him to come to her apartment to search for clues to Mara's whereabouts.

The alarms should have gone off when he entered the apartment building. It was a hovel, not the type of place you would expect to find a glamour queen like Crystal.

Martinez was lying in wait for him. The minute Crystal opened the door to the apartment, Martinez fired. In spite of the agonizing pain in his knee, Leif fired back, hitting Martinez in the shoulder. When Martinez dropped his gun, Crystal tried to flee, but Leif slammed the door. He held them both at gunpoint while he radioed for assistance.

His only comfort now was that they were both behind bars for a long time to come. The courts did not take kindly to people who shot at cops.

But Tracy was not another Crystal. Instead of fawning over him, Tracy actually tried to avoid him.

He barely focused on the rest of the service. He would just have to trust God to show him the way before he fell into another trap. His first mistake had only cost him his knee. This time it could cost him his heart.

The choir room was crowded after the service as the members hung up their robes and put their music away. Everyone congratulated Tracy on her solo.

"That was fabulous."

"I could listen to you sing all day."

"You made me cry."

Tracy looked overwhelmed by the attention, but she gave everyone her 500-watt smile. Leif watched fascinated. Whenever she smiled, a funny little hole popped into her cheek. He could have picked her up and kissed her right there in front of the whole choir.

Cool it, Ericson, he told himself.

"Tracy, are you really going to start a handbell choir?" one of the women asked.

Tracy looked hesitant. "I'm thinking about it. Rev. Jim said we have a five octave set of bells that someone donated years ago, but they've been sitting in the storage room ever since."

"Go for it," another member chimed in. "I'd love to play handbells."

Leif stood listening to the chatter when he felt someone clasp his arm. He looked down to see Sheila Dunn gazing dreamily into his eyes. No wonder Tracy thought this woman was his wife.

He edged his way through the crowd, ignoring the fact that Sheila was still firmly attached to him. "Tracy, your song was beautiful." Somehow the words weren't adequate to express how deeply the song had affected him.

But she smiled gratefully. "Thank you, Leif. That's my very favorite song."

"What time should I pick you up for work?" He tried to disregard the disapproving sniff from Sheila.

Tracy gave Sheila a curious glance. "I have to be there at four. I think three-fifteen should give us plenty of time."

"Three-fifteen it is."

"Thanks so much, Leif. I'll see you then, but I have to run now. Maggie's waiting for me."

Leif stood silent, his gaze following Tracy as she turned to the door. He felt Sheila tugging at his arm. He looked down to see her adoring gaze had become a disgruntled frown. "I don't understand you, Leif, making such a fuss over that woman. And why does Rev. Edwards let her in the door? Everyone knows she's a disgrace to this town."

Leif managed to escape Sheila's grasp as he removed his choir robe. He didn't feel the need to respond to her comments. If everyone knew Tracy was a disgrace, "everyone" didn't include Leif Ericson.

That New York detective, Diaz, had told him to keep an eye on Tracy in case Rick Timmons paid her a visit. He had done a thorough job of watching her, maybe too thorough, but so far there was no sign of a mysterious stranger. Still, he had to admit that watching Tracy Dixon was not a hardship.

****

Tracy studied her appearance in her mother's old cheval glass. The restaurant's pale blue uniform with white piping was attractive. She was really looking forward to this evening. She enjoyed waitress work, and it would be a relief to have money trickling in instead of pouring out.

Waiting on tables had paid her way through

three years of college, but her flight to New York sent her plans off on a detour. Even counting her evening classes at NYU, she still needed a full semester's credits to finish her final year and earn her degree in music.

Excitement bubbled up inside. "You can do it," she told her reflection. "Save enough money this summer, and you can enroll at Bridgewater for the fall semester. That degree will be in your hot little hand by the end of the year."

She was startled by a knock at the front door. That couldn't be Leif already. It wasn't quite three o'clock. She made a last quick check of her appearance and hurried downstairs to open the door. With Leif's warnings ringing in her head, she left the chain in place.

The middle-aged man on her doorstep was tall and painfully thin with a smattering of scraggly salt and pepper hair. A scar that ran down his cheek from his eyebrow to his chin shouted "Danger".

Tracy's heartbeat accelerated. Forcing her voice around the lump of panic in her throat, she managed to speak. "Can I help you?"

"Yes, Ma'am." The man gave her a toothless grin. "I hear you got a car for sale—a '74 Ford Galaxie, but I ain't seen it around for a while."

Tracy felt a faint glimmer of relief. He sounded so reasonable and matter of fact. But the break-in was still fresh in her mind. She needed to stay on alert. This could be a ruse to gain entry into her house. She looked past him to the rusted out Chevy he parked in her driveway. "The car is not for sale," she explained. She started to close the door.

The man shifted his weight from one foot to the other. "Can I take a look at it? I could probably make you a right good offer," he wheedled. "What about ten thousand dollars?"

Tracy stared at him. Why would someone pay that kind of money for an old car destined for the glue factory? "I'm sorry, but it's not for sale," she repeated. "You'll have to excuse me, I'm late for work." Quickly she closed the door and threw the deadbolt.

But the man didn't move. His voice came through the door. "I'd still like to look it over. What would you say to fifteen thousand?"

Fifteen thousand! He had to mean fifteen hundred. With fifteen thousand dollars she could buy a late model used car and have money left over. But this was ridiculous. The man didn't look as though he had fifteen dollars, let alone fifteen thousand.

"My car is in the shop for repairs," she called. "I do not wish to sell it and that's final." She waited quietly behind the door, hoping her silence would convince him to give up and go away.

After several minutes passed, she moved cautiously into the living room where she peered through the sheer curtains to get a view of the front yard. Apparently the man still stood on her doorstep. His battered car was still in the driveway.

She made a quick mental search of the house, trying to think of something to use as a weapon if he made an attempt to break in. The only thing that came to mind was the old tried and true standby—a rolling pin.

She glanced anxiously up at the clock. Five more minutes. "Hurry up, Leif," she whispered. "I could use some reinforcements."

****

Leif frowned as he approached Tracy's house. Why was that broken down heap parked in her driveway? Although her front door was firmly closed, a man stood on her doorstep. Leif knew he had never seen this character before.

Easing off on the accelerator, he rolled slowly past the house, sizing up the stranger. Was this the notorious Rick Timmons trying to contact his accomplice in crime, Tracy Dixon?

He pounded a fist on the steering wheel. *Just when I started to believe her.*

But Detective Diaz said Timmons was well built. This guy looked as though he had been on a hunger strike. And unless Timmons was a master of disguise, no one would accuse this man of being good-looking.

Without hesitation Leif swung a one-eighty and rolled to a stop in front of Tracy's home. Startled, the stranger glanced over his shoulder. One glimpse of Leif and he made a fast about face, beating a hasty retreat to his car. Before Leif opened his door, the man revved his engine and backed out of the driveway.

Automatically Leif jotted down the license plate number as the old Chevy took off toward town in a cloud of exhaust. He marched grimly to the front door. *Now let's see what this is all about.*

His knock was much heavier than necessary. "Tracy, it's Leif. Are you ready to go?"

Instantly Tracy opened the door. She stood there looking pale and shaken, but her chin was up in that "Don't tread on me" look. Still he knew her well enough by now to sense that she was frightened. He ached to pull her into his arms, but his brain took charge.

"I'm ready." Her voice was husky. "I'll get my purse."

Leif forced himself to wait until they were settled in the SUV before he questioned her. He sat behind the wheel without starting the engine. "Tell me about it." He studied her face for signs of guilt. All he could see was the lingering fear.

"Leif, I was scared." She clasped her hands in her lap as though to stop their trembling. "I don't know who that awful man was, but he said he wanted to buy my car. I can't believe he offered to pay fifteen thousand dollars for it."

"Fifteen thousand!" Leif exploded. "Either he's totally insane or he's playing some crooked game."

Tracy nodded. She seemed to be recovering her composure. "I knew that didn't make sense. I don't believe it was the car he really wanted. Do you think he's the man who broke into my house?"

Sorting through the possibilities, Leif turned on the ignition. "I got his tag number. Maybe that will tell us something. The fingerprints we took after the break-in were no help. All the prints Will lifted were either yours or Jeff's."

"I'm ashamed to be such a wimp," she apologized, "but that break-in left me hanging on by my fingernails."

A stranger would be terrifying to a woman alone in an isolated house that had just been invaded by a burglar. "That would drive anyone over the edge. You should get a dog."

Tracy managed a half-hearted laugh. "You sound like Maggie."

"Maggie's a smart lady," he reminded her.

As they drove through town, he sensed her uneasiness. He needed to take her mind off her strange visitor. "Can we drive into Boston Tuesday to see Jeff?"

"Leif," she protested, "you don't have to play chauffeur anymore. I should have my car back Wednesday."

"I'm not just playing chauffeur. I want to check on Jeff again. It doesn't make sense for us to drive to Boston in separate cars." What he didn't say was, I enjoy being with you.

She hesitated. "You're right. I just pray there's some sign of improvement. It's so disheartening to see him lying there, barely alive."

"Just try to remember that sense of peace we felt the last time we were there. I know God was telling us that Jeff would come through this." His words seemed to have the right effect. She sank back in her seat.

"Did you find Jeff's auto insurance information for Bradford?" He watched for her reaction to the mention of the lawyer's name.

"Yes, I found the policy. I need to drop it off at his office. Judge Whitby, the guardian ad litem, came to interview me Friday afternoon. I have a feeling he's not going to recommend me to be Jeff's conservator. I'm afraid I'll have to keep on putting up with Keith."

Leif suppressed a smile of satisfaction. So she didn't enjoy dealing with Bradford. That was a plus. He breathed easier as he turned the SUV into the parking lot at Fisherman's Landing. It was crowded on Easter Sunday afternoon. He drove as close as possible to the employees' side door entrance.

Tracy gave him a grateful smile. He felt that smile all the way down to his boots.

"Thanks for the millionth time, Leif. Maggie will pick me up after work. I won't need taxi service much longer."

Leif felt a jab of regret—not because that would reduce his chances of keeping an official eye on her, but because driving Tracy anywhere brightened his day. "You know you're always welcome."

"By the way," she teased, "if you're considering a career change, you can give Yellow Cab my name as a reference."

"You're so kind," he retorted as she climbed down from her seat. "I'll see you Tuesday."

He waited as she disappeared into the restaurant. He was a coward. He couldn't bring himself to tell Tracy that he turned down the court's request to act as Jeff Dixon's guardian ad litem. Of course, he didn't really know Tracy then. He had just met her, but he felt he was too personally involved with the family. Conducting a fair and impartial investigation wasn't possible. Based on hard cold facts, along with the rumors that circulated around her, how could he recommend her to the court?

So, Judge Whitby had taken on the job. The judge would have to be the one to shoot down her hopes.

Tracy Dixon, he thought, you've got me going in circles. I want to believe in you. Are you really an angel or just the best actress in Plymouth County?

CHAPTER IX

Tracy hesitated on the doorstep of Keith's office. Maggie dropped her off, but she would be back as soon as she filled her gas tank. If Tracy was in luck today, Keith would be out of the office. She had grown tired of fending off his amorous advances. She wanted to leave Jeff's auto insurance policy with his secretary and make a fast getaway.

She rang the bell and pulled the door open at the sound of the buzzer. Miss Collins sat at her desk busily typing on her computer. There was no sign of her boss.

Hallelujah. Tracy gave the secretary a cheerful grin as she laid the insurance policy on her desk. "These papers are for Mr. Bradford."

"Oh, Miss Dixon, let me tell him you're here."

"No, no, that's not necessary." Tracy backed away. "Just be sure that he ..."

She stopped in mid-sentence as the door to Keith's inner office swung open. She recognized the attractive woman who emerged - Keith's wife, Louise, with Keith right behind her.

Mrs. Bradford's face was on fire. "Do you ever stop to consider the consequences of your flirtations?" she snapped at Keith in an angry whisper. "Do you think you can win reelection if Senator Morris finds you've been making eyes at his wife?"

"Now, Louise that was just a little harmless

fun." Keith whined like a child who had to put away his toys.

Tracy stood frozen, embarrassed to be eavesdropping on a family squabble. But the quarrel came to a sudden halt as they noticed her presence. Their whole demeanor underwent a dramatic transformation.

Keith put on his dedicated attorney face. "Tracy, I didn't realize you were here. I think you know my wife, Louise."

Somehow Tracy dredged up a response. "Yes, but we've never been formally introduced. It's nice to meet you, Mrs. Bradford."

It was obvious that Louise Bradford was a politician's daughter. No one would guess that she had just been launching a tirade at her wayward husband. She gave Tracy a radiant smile and took her hand. "Oh, you're the girl with the beautiful voice. I can't tell you how much I enjoyed your song on Easter. Reverend Edwards should insist that you sing a solo every Sunday."

"Thank you. You're very kind." Tracy felt as though she had stumbled into No Man's Land, caught between two battling armies. She only hoped to make a graceful exit.

"I'm sorry that I have to run, but my friend is waiting for me. Keith, I left Jeff's insurance policy with Miss Collins."

"Good, wonderful!" he exclaimed, as though she had just reported some marvelous accomplishment. "I'll get right on it."

"Goodbye for now." She tried not to break into a run as she headed for the door.

Maggie waved to her from the cab of the old pickup parked at the curb. Tracy strolled down the walk with all the dignity she could muster. Did Louise Bradford know that Keith had once been her fiancé? She hoped Louise never discovered that Keith had been forcing his attentions on her. Mrs.

Bradford would never want to hear her sing another note in church again.

****

Jeff's condition seemed unchanged as Tracy and Leif stood gazing through the glass wall into his sterile prison. Tracy studied Jeff's face. Had the swelling lessened just a bit, or was she seeing what she wanted to see instead of reality?

Oh, Jeff, open your eyes or say something. A single tear rolled slowly down her cheek. She reached for Leif's hand. In spite of all her good intentions, she needed his strength. She couldn't see any sign of improvement.

But Dr. Burrows was smiling as he joined them at the window. Tracy dashed away the tear. *Please have some good news.*

"Miss Dixon, I'm very encouraged about your brother's progress. As you know we've done extensive skin grafts—his back, his legs, his arm, and his hands. We were able to use skin from his scalp and other areas that weren't damaged. It appears that at least ninety percent of the skin grafts have adhered."

Tracy's spirits soared. "Oh, bless you, doctor. That's wonderful."

"We're still keeping him in a coma, but he seems a little more responsive now. The next step is to take him to the tank to remove the burned tissue. That will promote the healing."

Tracy was sure she must be glowing like a candle. *Thank you, Lord. Thank you.*

Leif squeezed her hand. He looked as though a load had been lifted from his shoulders. He kept his feelings to himself, but Tracy suspected that inside he was suffering as much as she was.

She held tight to his hand as they stood in silence, just watching Jeff's immobile figure. Finally—a ray of hope. The first good news they had heard since the accident.

She was floating on a cloud as they returned to Leif's car. "I needed to hear that." Her joy bubbled over. "Even though we both felt God told us Jeff would be all right, I was getting so discouraged."

Leif nodded agreement. "It's hard to wait for an answer to prayer."

The sky was overcast with dull gray clouds hanging low on the horizon, but the world was beautiful. Tracy hummed a hymn to herself as they started the trip back to Allerton, "O What A Wonderful, Wonderful Day."

"Go ahead and sing it out loud," he urged.

She burst into full voice, putting her whole heart into the song. It expressed everything she was feeling. "Shadows dispelling, with joy I am telling, He made all the darkness depart."

Leif watched her with an amused smile. "You really love music."

She didn't have to mull over her answer. "Music makes me feel closer to God."

"So are you going to organize the handbell choir?"

"I couldn't resist. The church council gave me permission to order everything I need— some simple music, mallets, gloves for the ringers. Some of the ladies are going to make pads for the tables. And four people had already volunteered to ring before I made up my mind to do it."

He laughed. "That sounds like an ambitious project. Can you handle all that?"

She was probably out of her mind to take on a bell choir, but she was looking forward to it. "If I don't keep my mind occupied, I just sit and worry about Jeff.

"Where did you learn to play bells?"

Tracy suspected Leif might be asking questions just to be polite, but he seemed genuinely interested. "My church in New York had a handbell choir, and I fell in love with ringing."

"How many ringers do you need?"

"Thirteen or fourteen people can usually handle five octaves of bells." She eyed his broad shoulders and muscular arms. "You know I could use a couple of husky men for the biggest bells. How about giving it a try?"

Leif looked startled. "I don't read music very well," he confessed. "I learn my part in the choir anthems by ear."

"Not to worry. I know a way to make it easy for you to read the notes you'd be playing."

"Maybe I could work it into my schedule." He was definitely hedging.

Nag, nag. Tracy felt as pushy as a snake oil salesman, but she really needed some serious muscle in the group. The big bells got awfully heavy after an hour of rehearsal. "We'll be practicing the bells while Mark and Luke are at youth choir rehearsal. You're usually at church then anyway."

"I'll think about it," he grunted.

Suddenly, without warning, Leif slammed on the brakes. Tracy's head snapped forward as she was thrown against her seat belt. Stunned, she turned to stare at him.

His eyes were fixed on a spot off the road in the trees at the foot of an embankment. She turned her head. She could see it too—the rear bumper of a car, barely visible in the underbrush. A car had swerved off the road, swallowed up by the trees.

He was already halfway out the door. "I need to check this out," he called over his shoulder, running and sliding down the embankment.

On the edge of her seat she watched as Leif disappeared into the woods. Drawing a deep breath, she felt a sudden jab of pain in her side. The seat belt had probably saved her from being thrown through the windshield, but it clamped around her ribs like a vise.

In minutes Leif raced back up the slope,

unmindful of his bad leg. He snatched up his cell phone and punched in 911. She trembled with tension, but he was as calm and unemotional as if he were ordering groceries.

"Send troopers and an ambulance to southbound I-495, just south of Route 24. Car off the road in the trees. Woman unconscious at the wheel. Baby crying somewhere in the car. We'll need the jaws of life."

When the dispatcher had all the information, Leif rushed to the back of the SUV and pulled out a tire iron. Instantly he skidded back down the embankment.

Tracy sat dazed for a moment and then Leif's words began to sink in. *A baby. A baby!* She shoved the door open. Jumping to the ground, she raced down the slope behind him.

The hood of the sedan was folded in like an accordion against the trunk of a huge oak tree. She could see the unconscious woman wedged behind the steering wheel. Her face had been burned from the explosion of the airbag, but that may have saved her life. Faintly Tracy heard the frantic cries of an infant. But where was the child?

Leif tried to force a door open. The crash had bent the frame of the car. The doors were all jammed tight. It would take more than a tire iron to pry open one of the doors.

Desperate, she peered through the window. Where was that baby? Where were the muffled cries coming from?

"Stand back," Leif ordered. "I'm going to break a window."

She backed off a few steps as he swung the tire iron against the window behind the driver. The glass became a spider web of cracks. With several more heavy blows, he cleared the window frame of shattered fragments.

Now she could clearly hear the baby's hysterical

screams. Each shriek felt like a knife in her heart. She whispered a prayer. "Please let it be fear, not pain."

The impact of the crash forced the back seat of the car forward and tipped it downward. The baby seat had been pushed down almost out of sight against the back of the front seat. The child was trapped in his seat head down.

She felt Leif's gaze. There was a question in his eyes. "Tracy, I'm too heavy. If I climb in there, I'm going to crush that baby. If I lift you through the window, can you crawl in and try to get him out."

Too breathless to speak, Tracy nodded. He reached through the broken window, trying to brush away the scattered glass. He cupped his hands to give her a step up. "Watch out for those splinters."

But avoiding the splinters of glass was impossible. The sharp fragments were like needles pricking her palms and her knees as she crawled cautiously over the back of the crumpled rear seat.

Could she get close enough to un-strap the baby from his car seat without jamming it down even further? His little feet were kicking frantically at the air. So far, there were no signs of blood.

She stretched out flat to distribute her weight. Gently she petted the child's foot. "There, there, little guy. We're going to get you out of here," she soothed. The terrified screams eased into whimpering sobs.

She squeezed a hand down into the narrow space, groping to find the release for the straps that trapped the little one in place. Flying blind, she relied on her sense of touch.

"It'll be OK. It'll be OK." She tried not to let her frustration show in her voice.

She gasped in triumph as her fingers closed around the plastic buckle. Sobbing and hiccupping, the baby clutched at her arm as she found the release button. And then a snapping sound told her the straps had released. *Thank you, Lord.*

"Now, honey, I'm going to pull you out. I'll try not to hurt you," she explained. The infant didn't understand her words, but he seemed to understand her tone of voice.

Sliding her hands down again, she managed to grasp his arms. *Patience. Patience. Patience.* She edged him out of his seat and slowly began to lift him. *Careful. Careful. Careful.* A snag could tear his tender skin like a knife. He was heavy for such a little guy, but nothing stood in her way now.

At last, like a cork coming out of a bottle, he popped free. He continued to sob and whimper, but it was weariness not panic in his voice. Arms trembling from the strain, Tracy cuddled him as best she could in her awkward position.

Framed by the broken window, Leif watched her every move. "Great, Tracy. Perfect." He thrust his arms into the car. "Can you pass him to me?"

She managed to wriggle her way close to the window. Tears of relief rolled down her cheeks as Leif took the baby and carried him to a mossy spot on the ground. She barely had the energy to lift her head when Leif came back to the window to help her climb down.

She wanted to rest, but the baby started screaming again, frightened at being left alone. She dropped down on the ground and swept him into her arms. Cuddling and rocking him, she quieted his cries.

With his head inside the back window, Leif checked on the baby's mother.

"How is she?" Tracy worried.

"She's still unconscious, but I checked her carotid artery. She's got a strong pulse. We just have to hope there's no internal bleeding. Is the little guy OK?"

The baby was almost completely covered by his blue bunny pajamas, but Tracy checked for any signs of cuts or bleeding. He watched her with big, solemn, dark eyes. His breath came in deep, heavy gasps, but miraculously he appeared to be uninjured.

Tracy had to smile. "You're going to be a lady killer with those eyes," she told him.

Probably only ten minutes passed, but it seemed like hours before they heard the wail of sirens. The chill in the air began to penetrate Tracy's thin blouse. Hugging the baby close to keep him warm, she tried to stay out of the way of the horde of state troopers and paramedics who swarmed over the car. Leif worked with them as they struggled to force the car door open and free the woman.

There were grunts of triumph as the door gave way. As the paramedics eased the woman out of the car, she began to regain consciousness. Her eyes frantically searched the scene. "Michael. Baby," she whispered.

"He's here. He's OK." Tracy moved closer so the mother could see her little one. She managed a groggy smile.

Within minutes the paramedics were ready to carry the mother and child away. Reluctantly Tracy surrendered the infant to an EMT. Mother and baby—safe at last.

As they stood on the shoulder of the road, watching the ambulance drive away, Leif threw an arm around her shoulders. "Are you ready to go home now?" He spoke as though this incident was just a minor blip in his schedule, all in a day's work for him.

Drooping with exhaustion, she groaned. "You certainly know how to show a girl a good time."

He let out a whoop of laughter. "Yes, I always try to keep my lady friends entertained."

They trudged back up the embankment to the SUV. She barely had enough energy to climb into her seat, but Leif didn't drive away. He inspected the cuts in her hands and reached for his first aid kit.

"I'm sorry about the broken glass, Tracy, but you were an angel down there." Gently he dabbed disinfectant on the tiny wounds and then brushed her tangled hair back from her face.

She tried not to read too much into the tender touch. He was simply grateful for her help.

"You know, you are a handy lady to have around in an emergency," he teased. "Have you ever thought about joining the police force?"

"I think I had a nightmare like that once," she groaned. But the admiration in his eyes was all the medicine she needed to soothe her pain.

****

Leif tried to relax as he waited to speak to Keith Bradford. Although he had made an appointment, the attorney was still closeted with another client. He glanced impatiently at his watch. He didn't have much time to spare, but he was determined to find out, once and for all, what Keith knew about Tracy's past. Bradford had been the source of the rumors that tarnished her reputation in Allerton. If there was any basis for the insinuations, Bradford was the only one who held the answers to his questions.

Leif felt he had come to know Tracy well, and his experiences with her didn't fit into the picture Bradford painted of her mysterious misdeeds. Either Tracy had a split personality or she was innocent.

He started out playing "Mr. Nice Guy" with Tracy to discover the dark secrets behind that sweet innocent face. So far, he discovered that she was just as beautiful on the inside as the outside. But it's hands off for you, he reminded himself.

Bradford appeared at last, escorting an elderly lady. Leif waited until the woman was safely out the door and then stood as Bradford returned to greet him.

"Well, hello, Chief. Sorry to keep you waiting. Mrs. Stubbleford is a difficult client."

Leif shrugged and shook Bradford's extended hand.

"Come into my inner sanctum." The lawyer exuded charm and good cheer.

Leif followed him into the spacious private office. He had to admit that the rows of legal volumes that lined the walls were impressive.

Bradford waved him to a chair. "Now, what can I do for you today?"

Leif got straight to the point. "I want to ask you about Tracy Dixon."

Bradford's smile faded. "I assume you are investigating Tracy for some reason."

"I am," Leif said simply.

"I'm sure you are aware that Judge Whitby is already investigating Tracy as the guardian ad litem for Jeff Dixon. I understand that you turned down the appointment."

"I did," Leif admitted. "I felt that I was too personally involved with the family. But my questions don't have any connection with Tracy's petition to be named Jeff's conservator."

Bradford sat back in his swivel chair and folded his arms across his chest. "You understand that I am Tracy's attorney and that she is protected by attorney-client privilege. Any matters between us are strictly confidential."

"You weren't her attorney three years ago," Leif reminded him. "You were her fiancé."

Bradford didn't respond. His mouth hardened into a straight line.

"A number of people have told me that you spread the word around town that Tracy had been involved in some illicit activities. I've checked back through the records, but I can't find her name mentioned in any of the police reports."

"Well, of course, that shoplifting incident took place in Brockton."

"And is that incident the shady past you were

hinting at?"

Bradford gave him a sly wink. "Not every misdeed comes to the attention of the police."

Pinning Bradford down was as easy as nailing Jello to the wall. He was the ultimate politician. But Leif was determined to persist with his questioning. "Did these famous misdeeds include anything illegal?"

The lawyer drew himself up, the picture of injured dignity. "I don't think it's my place to be discussing Tracy's personal affairs."

"In other words, you don't have a shred of evidence to support your rumors and insinuations about her."

"I didn't say that," Bradford protested.

"Then tell me the basis for the stories."

"I repeat, I don't feel it's my place to be discussing Tracy's personal affairs. That's all I have to say." Bradford was stonewalling.

Leif had questioned enough suspects to recognize a bluff when he heard one. That hostile, defiant attitude meant Bradford was lying. There was no basis for his rumors about Tracy.

Abruptly Leif got to his feet. "Thank you for your time, Counselor. I'll see myself out."

He restrained himself from storming out of the room. He should have listened to Lucille from the start. Bradford circulated the lies about Tracy so he wouldn't look like such a rat when he broke their engagement.

And he had swallowed those rumors too. *You're an idiot, Ericson. You were as gullible as the rest of this town.*

At last, he didn't have to worry about the problems in Tracy's past, but what about the present? There was still the small matter of Ronda Starr's jewelry.

CHAPTER X

It was a glorious spring day. Tracy decided to forget about burglars and weird strangers and shadowy figures that might or might not be following her. She threw open the windows to inhale the haunting fragrance of lilacs. The bushes on either side of the front door were heavy with the pale purple blossoms.

You lived in the city too long, she thought. She had forgotten the wonderful sights and smells of the country in spring. The house was clean from top to bottom. It was time to do something about the yard.

With her wardrobe so limited, it was not a good idea to subject her clothes to yard work. Her roommate had sent off her clothes from New York, but the boxes had not arrived yet. A search of the ragbag produced a pair of her mother's old gardening pants—patched, re-patched and heavily stained. They were baggy, but she anchored them around her waist with a length of rope.

How about her brother's clothes? Jeff wouldn't mind, but there was a problem—he stood eight inches taller and at least eighty pounds heavier. His T-shirt covered her from neck to ankles like a nightgown.

She couldn't resist a glance in the mirror. Luckily there were no close neighbors to catch her looking like a hobo. *Just don't let this be the day Rev. Jim comes calling.*

Raiding the old shed in the backyard, she armed herself with gardening tools and began a survey of the property. Daisies sprang up along the low stone walls that marked the boundaries of the property. New England did not suffer from a shortage of rocks.

She stopped to admire the delicate apple blossoms in the neighboring orchard then got down to business. Her mother always kept a flower garden along the side of the house, but her plants had succumbed to neglect. Here and there a brave iris thrust its head through the weeds. The planter boxes under the windows showcased dirt instead of petunias and morning glories.

"I'll start with Mom's garden, but you're next," she promised the planter boxes.

She lost all track of time as she uprooted weeds and turned the soil. "This is my father's world," she sang cheerfully, feeling in tune with nature. One more weekend at Fisherman's Landing should give her enough money to invest in some seeds and plants.

It was nearing dusk when she heard the sound of an approaching car. She looked up to see Leif's SUV pulling into her driveway. Oh, no. Why did he have to show up now when she was on her knees looking like Dorothy's scarecrow in raggedy clothes, with every hair on her head blowing in a different direction?

Leif was usually so stoic, but he broke into a huge grin as he crossed the yard.

"Is this the elegant and fashionable Miss Tracy Dixon?" he teased.

She scowled at him.

He reached out to rub a smudge of dirt from her cheek. For such a big tough guy he could be so gentle.

"I have orders to deliver you to Maggie Scalia's," he announced.

"To Maggie's?" she puzzled.

"Instructions said, 'Do not take no for an answer.'"

"But—but—I can't go anywhere looking like this. I need a shampoo and a shower and clean clothes ... "

"I'll wait," Leif said calmly.

Too embarrassed to argue, she plodded meekly toward the door. Leif followed her into the house. "Maybe there's something on TV you'd like to watch," she suggested.

"Just go," he ordered.

"Yes, sir." She saluted him gravely and hurried up the stairs.

I'll bet that sneaky Maggie remembered it's my birthday, she decided as she rinsed her hair under the shower. But how did Leif get involved? If Maggie was playing matchmaker, her schemes would go down the drain when Leif decided to arrest Tracy.

She dried her hair and pulled on jeans and a blouse in record time.

Leif looked totally at home, relaxing in the recliner as he leafed through her high school yearbook. "That was quick. I thought we'd be here a while." He closed the book and got to his feet. "I see you were voted most popular girl at Allerton High School."

Tracy blushed, remembering the circumstances of that election. She had just been charged with shoplifting. "I think my friends voted for me just to irritate their parents," she confessed. "I wasn't too popular with the adults in town about then."

Leif insisted on following her around the house, peering over her shoulder as she locked up. No matter what he thought about her character, he was as protective as a secret service agent. Obviously, there would be no more burglaries on his watch.

The Scalias' house blazed with lights when they arrived. Maggie and Bud were waiting in their living room under an array of red and gold streamers and balloons. Our high school colors, Tracy remembered. A gigantic banner across the wall proclaimed, "Happy 26th Birthday."

Tracy hugged them both. "You are really sneaky. You wouldn't believe what I looked like when Leif came to get me. Thank goodness he didn't have a camera."

"The picture is etched in my memory," Leif announced solemnly.

"Don't worry about it. This is a come-as-you-are party," Maggie explained.

"If I came over dressed as I was, you would have locked all the doors and hidden in the kennels."

Maggie's dinner was a triumph. Tracy's very favorite foods—New England clam chowder and steamed Maine lobster. What more could anyone want?

"I hope you're not tired of lobster after working at the Landing," Maggie teased.

"It will never happen," Tracy assured her. "Serving them and eating them are not exactly the same thing."

"Maggie, you should open your own restaurant." Leif rubbed his stomach. "You'd put Fisherman's Landing out of business."

Tracy saw another side of Leif tonight. The stern, silent Viking kept them all in hysterics with stories about some of the inept criminals he had put away. Her eyes were riveted to the flash of those strong, white teeth and the crinkles of laughter around his eyes.

Even Bud, normally shy and introverted in complete contrast to his exuberant wife, added his share of strange stories about the misadventures of operating a kennel.

Tracy would have enjoyed sitting there all night, but she knew the Scalias were early risers. "Maggie, it's getting late. Let me help you clean up here."

"No, you're the guest of honor. You can clean up

when it's my birthday. Besides, Leif has a present for you."

"I'll be right back," Leif promised, disappearing out the back door. He returned leading a half-grown puppy on a leash. The animal's fur was a soft, silky brown. He pranced along beside Leif on the biggest feet she had ever seen. He looked like an awkward adolescent with too many arms and legs.

Tracy knelt to put her arms around the dog's neck. The puppy proceeded to wash her face with his tongue. His hindquarters wagged enthusiastically along with his tail. He gazed up at her with soulful brown eyes.

She was captivated. "Oh, Leif, thank you. He's so adorable. What breed is he?"

Bud eyed the puppy thoughtfully. "In my expert opinion, he's a dog."

Tracy giggled.

"I think he's mostly Golden Retriever," Maggie added, "with maybe a little Collie."

"I'm guessing he's got some German Shepherd in the mix," Leif suggested. "He'll make a good watchdog."

The dog didn't look ferocious enough to defend her against a rabbit, but she was in love with him at first sight. "Does he have a name?"

"It's your choice."

Tracy settled on the name of the Norse god of thunder. She knew the others wouldn't recognize the connection to Leif, her Viking. "I'll call him Thor."

As their gift Maggie and Bud contributed the food and equipment she would need. "He's had all his shots," Maggie assured her, "and he's housebroken—most of the time."

How can you thank friends like that? She hugged them goodnight. "You are absolutely the best friends in the whole world."

As Leif drove her home, Thor sat in the back seat, wearing a huge grin. Tracy bubbled over with plans for the puppy. "I have some old blankets that will make a perfect bed. Maybe I'll let him sleep in my room for now. I've never had a dog. Do you think I can teach him some tricks?"

Leif laughed. "The first trick you have to teach him is where to do his business. The next trick is to keep him from chewing up your shoes and your furniture. You can get around to 'sit, beg, and roll over' a little later on."

As Tracy led Thor on his leash, Leif escorted her to her front door lugging a supersized bag of puppy chow. "I'll feel better now that you're not alone in the house," he said gruffly.

Tracy looked up into those sea-gray eyes. "Thank you so much, Leif. This is the best birthday I've ever had."

For a long moment Leif stood silent, his gaze fastened on her face. Gently he reached out a hand and traced the curve of her cheek. Tracy held her breath.

Her birthday got even better as he lowered his head and pressed a soft kiss to her lips. Standing on tiptoe, she put her arms around his neck and melted into his embrace. This was crazy—he was a cop and she was America's Most Wanted —but it felt so right.

The kiss ended when Thor wrapped his leash around their legs.

****

The small handbell room was crammed with people and a floor full of bell cases. Thirteen ringers stood elbow to elbow behind the padded tables which were arranged to form a semi-circle around Tracy's music stand.

Leif pulled on his gloves and hefted the bells on the table in front of him. Although they were no problem for him, he understood why Tracy needed some muscle for these lower bells. Some of the smaller women would have trouble picking them up, let alone ringing them.

The lettering on his bells said F3 and G3. He had no idea what the markings meant, but Tracy told him he should hold the F bell in his left hand and the G bell in his right hand. She had circled the notes on his music with red and blue markers. A red circle meant ring the right hand bell; blue meant ring the left hand bell. That didn't sound too complicated.

Handbells for dummies, he decided.

Singing in the choir, he learned enough about music to recognize the various notes—an eighth, a quarter, a half, a whole note—and how many beats to hold each one. All he had to do was count. You can do this, he told himself.

He glanced around the room to see if anyone else looked as confused as he felt. Maggie was there, of course, but he was surprised to see that Sheila Dunn had volunteered to ring. Tracy was not one of Sheila's favorite people.

Tracy looked like a little schoolmarm behind the music stand. Her beautiful dark hair, pulled up in some kind of a fancy twist, made her look very dignified. He could tell that she was in her element, excited about this first rehearsal with her rag-tag ringers.

Get your mind off that kiss, he told himself. The memory of that night sent his pulse into overdrive. But he put on the brakes. He was in dangerous territory. No cop with a brain would get involved with a suspect, but she had cast some kind of a spell over him. How had she hypnotized him into joining a handbell choir?

Her sweet voice interrupted his musings. "Now, to make the bells sound their best, we don't just bang them." She shook a bell with a harsh clang. "To get a musical sound, we need to make circles with our hands, like this. It not only sounds better, it looks more dramatic." She demonstrated the correct way to ring. "Now, everybody try it."

Leif tried to make a circular movement with his hand, but he was beginning to have doubts about his coordination. Maybe his hands weren't connected to his brain. In his first attempt, he made a perfect circle, but no sound came out of the bell. With enormous patience, Tracy showed him how to flick his wrist as he began his circle.

When the group seemed to be getting the hang of it, she went on. "Now to stop the sound, we need to damp the bell by touching it to our shoulder or chest." She demonstrated again, ringing the bell with a graceful circling motion and then silencing the sound against her sweater.

They all tried ringing and damping.

"Now, everybody take a bell in each hand. Ring the bell in your right hand, damp the sound, and then ring the bell in your left hand. They shouldn't both ring at the same time."

After several minutes of ringing and damping, they were all anxious to try actually playing a song.

Tracy picked "Amazing Grace" as their first piece. "I tried to pick music that didn't have too many accidentals," she explained.

Accidentals? Leif puzzled. *Whatever they are.* He felt like an accidental waiting to happen.

Tracy gave them a count of three and they all plunged enthusiastically into the song. The result was total chaos. It sounded as though no two ringers were playing the same song.

Before they were halfway down the first page, Tracy signaled them to stop. She looked shell-shocked. "You have to count," she said patiently. "This is three-four time. Three beats to a measure. Don't hurry. It isn't a race to see who can finish first. When my baton comes down, that's beat one. You have to watch me."

Maggie spoke up. "Tracy, how many music directors does it take to change a light bulb?"

"Tell me," she said.

"Nobody knows." Maggie gave her a sly smile. "Nobody watches the director."

Leif smothered a laugh. Watching the music and the director at the same time was not easy.

"Very funny," Tracy scolded, but she joined in the laughter. "Now, let's try it again, watching and counting, watching and counting."

Leif was surprised at their second attempt. There were a number of goofs, including a few of his own but from time to time it was actually possible to recognize the song they were playing.

Tracy looked thrilled. "All right!" she exclaimed. "We're on a roll. Let's try it again. Remember your circles."

Despite a few miscues, by the fourth time through, the sound was fairly good. The choir gave itself a round of applause.

And then Leif felt his cell phone vibrating in his pocket. Carefully he laid his bells on the table and stepped out into the hall. "Chief Ericson," he said.

"Leland, it's Lucille. You better get over here fast. The alarms at Henry's garage are making an awful racket. I'll bet they can hear them down in Plymouth."

"I'm on my way. Who's on duty—Mike and Will? Tell them I'll handle it. And you'd better give Henry a call."

Leif put his head in the door of the music room. "Tracy, I have to go. If I don't get back in time, see that the boys get home."

Tracy waved an acknowledgment and Leif made a dash for his car. The minute he stepped out the door of the church, he heard the shrieks and clamor of the alarm. Henry had devised his own alarm system. It didn't send a quiet signal to some remote security company. It announced to the whole town of Allerton and points beyond, that someone was breaking into Henry's garage.

Jan Washburn

The garage was just a few blocks from the church. By the time he pulled up in front of the building, Leif decided that ear plugs should be standard equipment in his SUV.

Henry arrived at the same time. "Henry," Leif shouted to make himself heard over the din, "can you shut that thing off?"

Henry signaled an OK. Despite his hefty three hundred pounds, he sprinted to the office, unlocked the door, and disappeared inside. In an instant there was a blessed silence.

Immediately Leif began an inspection of the building. Although there were no signs of tampering on the garage bay doors, there were suspicious gouges in the wood frame of the office door and the striker plate had been bent back.

Henry leaned over Leif's shoulder as he examined the marks. "Looks like he tried to use a chisel or a screwdriver," he commented.

"What have you got in the safe, Henry? The crown jewels?"

"I don't even have much cash," Henry assured him. "I made a deposit at the bank yesterday."

"He must have been after your tools," Leif decided.

"There's nothing else there to steal," Henry put in. "I suppose maybe a car, if he wanted to smash it straight through the wall. He couldn't open those bay doors unless he brought a bolt cutter. Besides, the only cars in the garage right now are my old pickup truck and Tracy's Galaxie. Not exactly high priority for car thieves."

Leif examined the door again. "There's not too much damage to the wood, but you'll need to replace that striker plate."

Henry nodded. "I've been in business here for thirty years. First time something like this happened. I'm glad he didn't get my tools."

"Reset your alarm," Leif reminded him. "I have a

feeling this guy is going to come back." He stood for a moment, studying the scene. "Henry, I don't like the smell of this. There's something fishy going on here."

CHAPTER XI

Leif tilted his chair back and stared at the office ceiling. It had been several days since the attempted break-in at Henry's, but something about it kept gnawing at the fringes of his mind. Absent-mindedly he massaged his bad knee as he tried to diagnose the source of his unease.

A thief should know that Henry didn't keep a lot of cash on hand. People paid for car repairs with a check or credit card, not petty cash. If a crook was looking for a place to steal tools, Henry's garage was not the best choice. It was built like a fortress. Robbing the hardware store would be as simple as a rock through a plate glass window.

As for stealing Henry's pickup truck or Tracy's Ford—there were easier places to grab a car. There was nothing else of value in the garage unless Henry had some special equipment that he had overlooked.

His musings were interrupted by a commotion outside his office door. He jumped to his feet, afraid that Lucille was climbing on a chair again to change a light bulb. Yanking the door open, he found Will forcing a seedy looking man into a chair as Lucille prepared to book him.

"What's up, Will?"

"I didn't do nothing wrong," the man shouted.

"Old man Miller found this guy sleeping in his shed," Will reported. "Doesn't think he stole anything."

Leif studied the vagrant with suspicion. He had seen this man before. A picture came into his mind of the stranger who came to Tracy's door offering to pay fifteen thousand dollars for her old Ford. He caught only a brief glimpse of the man that day, but the image was clearly imprinted in his brain. Tracing the license plate on the guy's junk Chevy had led to a dead end. The plate had been stolen from another car in Wareham.

But this was definitely the same man—painfully thin, scraggly hair. He was even wearing the same nauseous green sweatshirt.

"I believe I've met this gentleman before, Will. Before you book him, I'd like to have a little talk with him." Leif turned to the culprit. "What's your name?"

"John Sylvester."

"Any aliases?"

"No, sir. I ain't no crook."

"You'd better be telling me the truth," Leif warned. "Lucille, run that name through the system."

"Of course, Leland."

"I'll take care of this, Will. Mr. Sylvester, if you'll please step into my office."

Impeded by the handcuffs behind his back, the prisoner managed to unfold to his full height. He slouched into Leif's small office and dropped heavily into a chair.

Leif was more interested in the man's visit to Tracy than in the trespassing charge, but he started with the immediate problem. "So what were you doing in Mr. Miller's shed?"

The man's voice was thin and reedy, almost a whine. "I been trying to pick up some work. Make enough money for bus fare home. That place looked as though they could use a handyman, but there weren't nobody home. I waited a while, but no one showed. When it started to rain, I ducked in the shed. I didn't mean to fall asleep." Sylvester's voice trailed off. He looked expectantly at Leif, obviously hopeful that his sad tale of woe would earn him a little sympathy.

"Where's home?"

"Portland, Maine. Never shoulda left."

Leif pretended to be mulling over a decision, although he knew exactly where he was going with this. He stroked his chin thoughtfully. "Well, I might be able to forget the trespassing in exchange for some information."

Sylvester frowned. "Information? I don't know nothing."

"We'll see." Leif smothered a smile. "A week ago you knocked on a lady's door offering a ridiculous amount of money to buy her car. Tell me what that was that all about."

Sylvester came to attention. "That ain't illegal."

"No, that's true, but those were stolen tags on your car."

"That weren't my car," he protested. "I swear. A guy loaned it to me. I didn't know the tags was stolen."

"And where were you planning to get fifteen thousand dollars to pay the young lady for her car?"

Sylvester shifted uneasily in his chair. Leif knew the handcuffs were making him uncomfortable, but he suspected they weren't the source of Sylvester's uneasiness. The vagrant eyed him cautiously. "You're gonna forget the trespassing if I tell you about that?"

"I said I might do that."

Sylvester seemed to be holding a debate with himself. To tell or not to tell. He heaved a deep sigh. "I wasn't really gonna buy the car. This guy in Wareham said he'd pay me a hundred bucks if I'd find out where the lady's car was. I figured the easiest way to find out was to just go and ask the lady."

Leif hesitated. This story wasn't making a whole lot of sense. "Why did this guy want to know about the car?"

The vagrant shrugged. "Don't ask me. All I cared about was making a hundred bucks."

"Do you know the man's name?"

He shook his head. "No idea. The church serves a free lunch on Saturday. I was sitting there, eating my lunch, minding my own business, and this guy just walked in and picked me out of the crowd."

"What did he look like?"

"I don't know. Just a guy. About thirty or so. Tall, dark hair."

"Had you ever seen him before?"

"Nope. Never laid eyes on him."

"And that's all the description you can give me?" Leif snapped.

"Well, he was dressed nice. Real classy looking. Had a little beard, you know what I mean, like he forgot to shave."

"Did he give you the money up front?"

"No, he gave me twenty-five. Said he'd give me the rest when I had the information for him. He gave me two days to find out—said he'd meet me behind the church on Monday evening." Sylvester frowned in disgust. "I had to spend twenty bucks to get the loan of the car."

"So, did this guy come back and meet you?"

"Yup. He showed up and paid me the seventy-five bucks. But he told me I better keep my mouth shut about the whole deal or he'd hunt me down. He looked like he meant what he said."

Leif was silent, pondering the story. There had to be a reason the mystery man didn't call on Tracy himself. He paid good money to a total stranger when all he needed to do was knock on Tracy's door. And then Leif felt a familiar tingle at the back of his neck. He had a hunch.

He stepped to the door. Will was still outside,

waiting for further orders. Leif opened his wallet and handed him a fifty. "Will, I want you to take this gentleman to Brockton and put him on the bus to Portland. There should be enough money there to buy him a meal."

Lucille's mouth fell open and Will stared at him in astonishment. "What about the trespassing charge?"

"Mr. Sylvester was kind enough to assist me with another case. We're going to overlook the trespass."

"Yes, sir." Will shrugged as though there was no point in arguing with someone who was clearly insane. Reluctantly he removed Sylvester's handcuffs and escorted him out to the patrol car.

The last thing Leif heard was the hobo's plaintive voice, "My back pack's still in that shed."

Leif gave Lucille a wink and returned to his desk. Ideas bounced around in his head like ping pong balls. The mystery man had to be Rick Timmons. Knowing Tracy would recognize him, he sent a stranger to get the information—a stranger who didn't know him, who couldn't be connected to him. But why was Timmons interested in Tracy's car? There must be something special about that old Galaxie.

Leif's suspicions began to take shape. He opened a desk drawer and pulled out the Timmons file. Detective Diaz had faxed the list of jewelry stolen from Ronda Starr's home. He scanned the list of items. There were detailed descriptions of each piece—a twenty carat solitaire, a gold choker, an antique brooch set with rubies and emeralds. There were eight pieces in all. Leif trusted his instincts and they told him that Timmons had stashed a small fortune in jewelry in Tracy's car.

The very idea sounded like something out of Mad Magazine. But more often than not his crazy hunches were on target. He paused, jolted by another thought. A bigger question loomed—if that jewelry was in Tracy's car, did she know it? He didn't want to believe that.

"Lucille," he called. "I need to talk to Henry."

"I'll get him, Leland."

Leif shoved the file back into the drawer, his mind racing at warp speed. To prove his hunch he needed to be careful. If he made an illegal search, he jeopardized the case. He had to talk to Tracy before he touched her car.

"Henry's on the line," Lucille called.

Leif snatched up the phone. "Henry, have you called Tracy to tell her that her car is ready?"

"Not yet. I just finished some final adjustments. I'm just getting ready to call her."

"OK. This is important. Tell her I'm on my way out there to get her. I want to be with her when she comes to pick up that car."

****

Tracy held the phone between her ear and her shoulder as she tried to persuade Thor to chew on his rag doll instead of the coffee table. She had discovered that puppies were hazardous to clothing, furniture, and anything else that didn't move fast enough. To protect Pansy Panda, she moved her stuffed childhood friend from the place of honor on her pillow to the top shelf of her bookcase.

"Hi, Mom," she said as her mother answered her call. "How's Aunt Grace doing?"

Her mother tended to see the gloomy side of life. "Well, the doctor says she's doing fine, but I don't know. She doesn't seem to have much pep."

"Mom, she just had a triple bypass. She needs a lot of rest."

"I know, I know," her mother fretted, "but she doesn't have much of an appetite, and Grace has always been such a good eater."

Tracy tried to bolster her mother's spirits. "Just give her some time. Everyone here at church is praying for her and for Jeff."

At the mention of Jeff's name, Faith grew weepy. "Oh, my poor boy."

"Mom, don't give up." Tracy wanted to instill in her mother the feeling of peace she had about Jeff— that wonderful sense of God's presence telling her that all would be well. "There's some good news. The doctor is really encouraged about the way the skin grafts are adhering."

Her mother's answer was interrupted by a knock at the door. "Hold on a minute, Mom. Someone's at the door." Tracy put the phone down. Remembering to leave the chain in place, she opened the door a crack. Joy bubbled up. There stood Leif. But the bubble burst when she saw his grim expression.

She removed the chain and opened the door. His frown gave her prickles of anxiety. "Hi, Leif. What's up?"

Thor danced up to the door, trying to win his attention, but Leif didn't seem to be aware of the puppy. His penetrating gaze searched her face. "Didn't Henry call you?"

She shook her head. "I guess he couldn't reach me. I've been on the phone." She decided not to mention that Keith Bradford had called. He had located the charred remains of Jeff's car. She knew Leif shared her aversion to Keith.

"Your car is ready. I told Henry I'd bring you in to pick it up."

"That's great! At last," Tracy cheered. But Leif was scowling as though he were bringing her bad news.

She waved him into the house. "Come in a minute while I finish this call." As he followed her into the living room, she picked up the phone again. "Mom, I'm sorry, I've got company. Keep praying and keep your chin up. I'll call you back tonight."

"Don't forget," her mother chided.

"I'll call," Tracy promised. She hung up the phone and turned to Leif. "Just let me take care of Thor. He loves playing with the toilet paper roll. I'll put him in the kitchen. He can't get into too much trouble there."

When Tracy returned, Leif was pacing the living room floor. He was usually as excitable as a rock, but today he seemed to be on edge. "I'm ready," she ventured.

He held up a hand in a signal to stop. "Before we go, I need to ask you a few questions."

Tracy felt a knot forming in the pit of her stomach. Leif was acting so strangely.

"Sit down for a minute." This was a cop talking, not a friend.

Hesitantly she sank down onto the sofa. *Something is very wrong.*

"On the night you went to Ronda Starr's party, where was your car?"

Tracy felt her mouth drop open. She had managed to push the jewelry theft to a distant corner of her brain. And what did her car have to do with anything? "It was in the parking lot behind my apartment in Brooklyn."

"And Rick Timmons lived nearby?"

Now they were back to Rick Timmons. She struggled to follow Leif's train of thought. "I don't know exactly where Rick lives, but I'm sure it was somewhere nearby in the neighborhood."

"Did you always park in the same place?" This wasn't a conversation, it was a quiz.

"Yes, it's my assigned space. I pay to park there."

"Is the parking lot fenced? Is there a security guard?"

She felt as though she were back in that dingy interrogation room with Detective Diaz. "There's a fence and a twenty-four hour attendant at the gate. The attendants can see anyone that comes through the pedestrian entrance and any car that comes in or out through the gate. And there are several security cameras around the lot."

"So the attendant would know if a stranger entered the lot."

"Well, not necessarily. It's not always one of the regulars on duty."

"So a stranger could enter the lot?"

The questions were endless. "A stranger could get in, but the attendant can see what's going on. Monitors show him what the security cameras are focusing on. Besides, no one could take a car out of the lot. We each have our own remote to open the gate."

Leif paused, but there was more. "When you came home from Miss Starr's party that night, did you check on your car?"

Tracy shrugged. "There was nothing to check. I saw it there in the parking lot. I just went to bed. Leif, why are you asking me these questions?"

"I'll explain later," he said tersely. "After that night, when was the first time you used your car?"

Tracy thought back. "The next morning, Sunday, I had to go to the police station, but they sent a patrol car to pick me up. Then on Monday I got the call from Maggie about Jeff's accident. I threw some clothes in a suitcase, jumped in the car, and left town. About eleven o'clock, I think."

"Were there any signs that someone had tampered with the car?"

Tracy frowned, trying to remember. "I didn't notice anything unusual."

Abruptly Leif stood up. "All right, let's go."

The knot in Tracy's stomach grew painfully tight as they drove to Henry's garage. Leif was silent, his jaw set firmly in concrete.

Henry greeted them as they walked into the garage through the open bay doors. "I'll bet you thought you'd never see your car again," he joked.

Tracy smiled, but Leif was all business. "Henry, I want you to listen to what I'm going to say to Tracy."

Henry looked as surprised as Tracy felt. "Sure," he agreed.

"Miss Dixon," Leif said formally. "Do I have your permission to search your car?"

Search her car? *For what?* "You have my permission," she murmured.

She stood mesmerized, watching as Leif began a thorough search of the old Ford. He started in the trunk, pulling up the carpeting and digging under the spare tire. He lifted the hood and studied the engine. He pawed through the glove compartment and peered under the front seat. And then he pulled out the back seat cushion. She heard his grunt of triumph. He paused to pull on a pair of latex gloves, and then reached down to remove a battered leather case. It looked like a smaller version of an attaché case. Tracy gaped at Leif's find.

He laid the case carefully on the hood of her car and tried to open it. The case was locked. He turned to Tracy. "Do you have the key?"

Tracy shook her head in bewilderment. "Leif, I never saw that case before in my life. It must belong to my mother, but I can't imagine why she would put it under the seat."

"Do I have your permission to break the lock?"

"Yes, of course." She hoped the contents weren't fragile. Her mother would fall into a dramatic swoon.

"Henry, I need a hammer and a screwdriver."

Henry thrust the tools into Leif's hands. Carefully Leif inserted the screwdriver into the seam next to the lock. A few quick taps with the hammer and the case sprung open.

All Tracy could see was what looked like rags inside the case, but Leif examined the objects wrapped in the cloths. He looked up at Tracy with those stormy eyes. "Miss Starr's jewelry," he said flatly.

Tracy felt her heart hit the soles of her feet. "What?" Her head reeled. If she didn't sit down, she was going to black out. This was unreal. She had actually driven that car from New York to Allerton with Ronda Starr's priceless jewelry inside. Groping for a seat, she found a pile of tires. "Are you—are you going to arrest me?"

Leif didn't answer her question. He looked directly into her eyes as though he were trying to read her thoughts. "You didn't know this jewelry was in your car?"

"Leif, I swear I had no idea." She dropped her head down into her hands to fight the waves of dizziness.

"I have to take this back to the station," he said without any trace of emotion. He placed the case into an evidence bag and then aimed a fierce look at her. "I don't want anyone else to know that the jewelry has been found. Not a word to anyone. Tracy, you don't tell Maggie. Henry, not even your wife. Do you understand?"

"I hear you," Henry responded.

Tracy nodded weakly.

Leif gave her one last glance. "Tracy, I'll be at your house in an hour. Henry, don't let her drive that car until she's feeling better."

Tracy gazed helplessly after Leif as he strode from the garage holding Ronda Starr's treasure and her future in his hands.

CHAPTER XII

Cradling the evidence bag in his arms, Leif entered the police station through the back door. Lucille was on the phone, as usual. Impatiently he tapped his foot until she finished.

"Lucille, hold my calls. I don't want to be disturbed unless the station is on fire or there has been a murder."

His right-hand lady gaped at him in astonishment. It took a lot to surprise Lucille. She had probably seen and heard everything in her day. "Yes, Leland," she managed.

Locking the door behind him, Leif laid the bag on his desk. His pulse raced as he opened the Timmons file and pulled out the fax with the list of Ronda Starr's missing jewelry.

Pulling on his gloves again, he unwrapped the items in the case. One by one he matched each piece to Diaz's checklist. Diamond tennis bracelet, Vacheron Constantin watch, antique brooch with rubies and emeralds, star sapphire ring, diamond earrings, twenty carat diamond solitaire, gold choker, art deco bracelet. The eight pieces were all there.

With a groan, he wrapped the pieces again and placed them back in the leather case. The case went into the evidence bag. He hoped the whole thing would fit into his small office safe. He wouldn't breathe easy until this small fortune was safely back in Miss Starr's hands.

Dialing the combination to the safe, he edged the bag inside. A close fit, but the treasure was as secure as possible for now.

He dropped into his chair. Now he had to call Diaz, but he hesitated. Before he contacted the detective, he had to know where Tracy fit into the picture. The stunned look on her face when he found the jewelry seemed completely genuine. But her shock could be due to fear of a prison term.

Still, he couldn't make himself believe she was a criminal. The pieces of the puzzle didn't fit together. If she was involved, why would Timmons have to trick her into revealing the location of her car? He would have no reason to break into Henry's garage to get the jewelry.

And Leif knew something about basic human nature. A jewel thief wouldn't spend her free time at church, singing like an angel and leading a handbell choir. She wouldn't be worrying about her family, visiting her brother and calling her mother. She wouldn't be soothing a frightened baby or a seven-year-old boy. She would be in Boston looking for a place to fence those jewels. There was only one way to prove her innocence.

He picked up the phone and punched in Diaz's number. The familiar raspy voice answered. "Detective Diaz."

"Chief Ericson here. I have Ronda Starr's jewelry."

"You what?" Diaz's voice shot up a full octave.

"I have Miss Starr's jewelry here in my office. Send someone to get it, pronto. My safe isn't exactly a bank vault."

Diaz seemed to be having trouble catching his breath. "You've got the jewelry? Did you get Timmons too?"

"No, not yet, but he's definitely somewhere here in the neighborhood."

Diaz grunted. "I don't know if you got the word. Ronda Starr's butler didn't survive the beating. Now we're looking for a murderer. If you didn't nab Timmons, how did you get the jewelry?"

Leif forced the words out of his mouth. "It was hidden under the back seat of Tracy Dixon's car."

Diaz whooped in triumph. "I knew that little con artist was in on the theft."

"I'm not so sure," Leif protested. "I don't think she knew it was there." How could he convince the detective? "I have a theory. I think Timmons stashed the jewelry in Tracy's car that same night it was stolen. He figured that if you caught up with him, you couldn't find anything in his possession to connect him to the theft. If you did find the jewelry, all the suspicion would fall on Tracy. Timmons must have decided to wait a day or two to let things cool down before he went back to get the jewelry, but by the time he got there, Tracy and the car were gone."

"Go on," Diaz said, his voice heavy with skepticism.

"The day after Tracy arrived here in Allerton, her car threw a rod. It was towed to the shop for repairs. A week later her house was broken into and ransacked, but nothing was taken. We couldn't figure out what the burglar might have been looking for."

"Hmm," Diaz muttered. He didn't sound impressed.

Leif hurried on. "Then a stranger came sniffing around, wanting to look at the car. He said he was interested in buying it. Tracy told him it was in the shop for repairs. This morning we picked up the man who asked about the car. He claimed some guy gave him a hundred bucks to find out where it was. Why would anyone pay a stranger a hundred bucks to locate a '74 Galaxie?"

"Go on," said Diaz.

Leif hoped the detective was buying his theory.

"It took me a while to put the pieces together. The guy with the money had to be Timmons. He was trying to find the car, but he couldn't ask the questions himself because Tracy would recognize him. Once Timmons found out that the car was in the repair shop, he took the next step. There was an attempted break-in at the shop, but the alarms scared the burglar away. When I put all the pieces together, I got Tracy's consent to search her car."

Diaz snorted. "Well, consent or not, you have grounds to get a warrant and take Miss Dixon into custody."

"Hold on, Diaz," Leif argued. "Think about it. You can't announce to the world that the jewelry has been recovered. That will blow any chance we have to catch Timmons. As long as he doesn't know we've already found it, he's going to keep trying to retrieve it. If I arrest Tracy, he'll know the party is over. He'll drop quietly off the face of the earth. No one will see or hear from him again. Even if Tracy is involved, she's small fry. We've got to nail the big fish."

"But if you leave her on the loose, she can get word to Timmons—head him off. He'll disappear and let her take the rap alone."

"We've got to take that chance," Leif argued. "It's the only way to trap him."

"All right, Ericson. You're making sense. We'll do it your way. I'll send an officer for the jewelry, but we'll keep it out of the news. But if your scheme doesn't net the big fish, I'm coming after your lady friend."

****

Tracy stared at the sandwich on her plate, but her stomach protested. She couldn't make herself swallow a bite. Leif was coming and she knew he didn't believe her. She tried to imagine what it would be like to be locked in a cell.

Thor chased a ball around the kitchen, his big feet slipping and sliding on the tiles, but she couldn't even smile at his antics. She hoped that Leif could see through Keith's rumors about her dishonesty, but once again a man had let her down. The new life she was trying to build was crumbling around her.

Leif had to believe she was guilty with that incriminating evidence staring him in the face. She had no way to prove that she had never laid eyes on that jewelry.

She froze as she heard his knock. It took all her will power to get up and open the door to Leif. "Come in," she managed.

His face was still set in that impassive expression—his mouth a grim straight line. It looked as though his features had been chiseled out of solid rock. Silently she waved him to a chair. Would he use handcuffs to arrest her or let her surrender peacefully?

He sat down in the living room as though this were a social call. "Tracy, I'm going to need your help."

"My help?" His words were so unexpected, she could barely speak.

"I believe that you did not know that jewelry was stashed in your car. That means Timmons hid it there and now he's trying to get it back."

Tracy was torn between elation that Leif believed her and confusion about the situation. "But why...why would he put it in my car?"

"Can you think of a better place?"

She could see Leif's logic. Her car had been parked in a convenient location for Timmons. If the police found the jewelry, she would be the goat.

"But how?" she puzzled. "I mean, there's an attendant at the parking lot gate all the time."

"Any smart crook could have found a way in. Maybe there was a new attendant on duty. Maybe he followed another tenant through the gate, acting as though they were together. It doesn't matter."

"But the security cameras?" She always thought

the cameras were all the protection anyone needed.

"Timmons was no dummy. He broke into your car on the side away from the cameras. With an old car like yours, he timed the sweep of the cameras and popped the locks in seconds."

"So how did he find me here in Allerton?"

"Did you warn your roommate not to tell anyone where you were going?"

Tracy bristled. "No, of course not. I knew the police would call, and I wanted them to know I wasn't trying to run away."

"And Timmons knew your phone number?"

Tracy hesitated. Did she give Rick her number? She nodded slowly. "Yes, I gave it to him that night—the night of the party."

"So when Timmons realized your car was gone, he made a quick phone call to your roommate and found out you were in Allerton. But when he arrived here, he discovered another problem. The Ford was still missing."

Instantly Tracy knew what Leif was thinking. "So he broke into my house. And when he didn't find the jewelry, he sent that weird man to find out where my car was."

Leif nodded solemnly. "Right. And Timmons isn't going to rest until he gets his hands on that jewelry."

She felt ice water trickle down her spine. "You mean he's going to keep trying to break into my car."

"That's what we're dealing with," Leif said flatly. His voice contained no more emotion than if they were discussing the weather. "It's our best chance to catch him. He might lie low for a while after failing to get into Henry's garage, or he might try again any time."

"But what can we do?" She wanted to fight back, but they were playing hide and seek with a phantom.

"We'll have to keep the car under surveillance.

I'm going to have my men patrolling past your house as much as possible. And I'll tip off the security guard at the Landing to be on alert when you're at work. But most of the burden of keeping watch is going to fall on you."

Tracy tried to imagine how to live a normal life while she kept one eye on her car 24/7. "I wish the Ford had an alarm system."

"Keep the car locked at all times. It won't stop Timmons from getting in, but it may slow him down enough to give us a chance to get him."

She nodded.

"Now this is important. I don't want you to put yourself in any danger. Don't try to confront him. If you see someone hanging around your car, call me. Day or night. I don't care if it turns out to be a false alarm. I want to nail this guy."

"Oh, Leif, so do I." Timmons had caused her enough grief to last a lifetime. "I'll do everything I can."

"I've put several pieces of tape against the seat cushion so we can tell if it has been moved." Leif stood up, his expression still stern and solemn. "There's just one last thing. If Timmons manages to get into your car without being seen and finds out his loot is gone, I will have to take you into custody for your own protection. He'll assume you have found the jewelry, and then he'll come after you."

Long after Leif left, she stood staring out the window. She felt trapped in a never-ending nightmare.

****

The handbell rehearsal was going beautifully. Tracy found joy in focusing on something besides her car. She had parked in the most visible space in the church parking lot. A church member would be bound to notice if someone tampered with the old Ford.

Her ringers now played "Amazing Grace" like

pros. Of course, it was an easy arrangement, but they were also making progress on another easy song, "Rock of Ages." Maybe they were ready to try something more difficult. The arrangement of "In My Heart There Rings A Melody" called for the use of mallets. Maybe her ringers were ready to juggle mallets along with their bells.

She gazed around at her faithful crew. They all loved music, and she felt that they loved her too, with a couple of notable exceptions. Sheila Dunn despised her, but at least she attended practices faithfully and did her best to learn.

But Tracy's spirits sank as she glanced at Leif. This wasn't the man who held her while she cried outside her brother's hospital room. This wasn't the man who gave her that melting kiss on her birthday. He said he believed in her innocence, but his actions out-shouted his words. Ever since the night he pulled Ronda Starr's jewelry out of her car, he wore a mask, concealing his emotions. Like Sheila, he never missed a rehearsal, but he concentrated on his bells, rarely speaking, avoiding meeting her eyes. An unbiased observer would think they were total strangers.

She blinked away a tear and lifted her chin. Let him disguise himself as a stone wall. She would not let another man hurt her. She would carry on as though Leif Ericson was the least important thing in her life.

"There's no worship choir rehearsal tonight," she reminded her ringers, "so we can take a few extra minutes. Let's run through 'Amazing Grace' one more time."

As they rang the last chord, she heard a round of applause coming from the hall outside the bell room. Rev. Jim strolled in, his face beaming. "That sounded great," he enthused. "I love it. Are you ready to play for the congregation?"

Tracy turned to the group. Most of them nodded

enthusiastically, but several of them looked a little panicky. "Give us one more week," Tracy decided.

"Good enough. You're on the program for a week from Sunday."

"Can everyone be here then?" Tracy asked. "If someone is missing, we've got a problem."

They all assured her they would be there for the service. It cheered her to hear them chatting and laughing as they polished their bells and put them away in the proper cases.

Tracy caught sight of Mark and Luke in the hall waiting for Leif. She waved to the boys and they rewarded her with their shy smiles. "We're just about finished," she called.

And then the babble was interrupted by a scream. The room fell silent as everyone stared at Sheila. "My ring," she gasped. "My opal ring is gone."

"Gone!" Tracy echoed. "It must be right here somewhere. Did you accidentally pull it off when you took off your gloves?"

Sheila checked the area around her while the others began a search of the tables and the floor.

"Are you sure you had it on when you came in?" Maggie spoke up. "When do you remember seeing it last?"

Sheila teetered on the verge of tears. "I took it off in the restroom when I washed my hands." And then she turned an accusing eye on Tracy. "You were the only other person there. And you were still in the restroom when I left."

Tracy's cheeks burst into flame. *Not again. Round up the usual suspects.*

"Sheila," she said firmly. "I did not see your ring. I did not touch your ring. It's probably right where you left it."

Maggie leaped to her defense. "A couple of you come with me. We'll check the restroom." Three ringers joined Maggie as she stormed out the door.

While the others kept searching on their hands

and knees, Sheila stood, arms folded, glaring at Tracy. Tracy glanced at Leif. Like the others he was hunting for the ring, probing through the bell cases, his face impassive. If he really believed she was innocent of the jewelry theft, this would change his opinion in a hurry.

Maggie looked dejected when the search party returned. "No luck. We went through the whole place. We even emptied the waste paper basket."

Tracy's hopes went into a downward spiral. She was sure Maggie would return in triumph.

But Maggie still pleaded her case. "No one here is a thief, Sheila. I'm sure you'll find it."

"I wouldn't count on it," Sheila snapped. "Leif, aren't you going to do something?"

Tracy held her breath, waiting for his answer.

"I am doing something," he said quietly. "I'm looking for it."

With a snort, Sheila stamped out of the room. One by one the other ringers gave up the search. They murmured words of sympathy and patted Tracy's shoulder as they left. Maggie gave her a fervent hug. "The ring will turn up," she insisted.

Leif was the last to leave. He paused and for a long moment, gazed into her eyes. His face was unreadable.

Had he reached his verdict—guilty as charged?

He put his hand on her shoulder and let it rest there a moment.

"Don't let Sheila get you down. She has her own agenda."

Did she hear sympathy in his voice? But she stood there feeling helpless as he too left the room. How could you regain your good name when everything and everyone seemed to be conspiring against you?

She closed her eyes and whispered a prayer. "Dear Lord, you know my heart. That should be enough for me. I shouldn't care what others think, but it hurts to know people believe I am a thief. Your word says, 'A good name is more desirable than great riches.' Please help me find a way to prove to the world that I am innocent."

CHAPTER XIII

Leif forced himself to walk out the door. Mark and Luke stood waiting for him in the hall, passing the time with a game of scissors, rock, paper. "Let's go, guys." He rounded up the boys and herded them out to the SUV. But instead of starting the engine, he sat motionless, watching Tracy's car.

If Timmons was following her, learning her schedule, he would know that on most Wednesday evenings she was tied up for almost three hours with handbell and worship choir rehearsals. That timetable would give Timmons plenty of time to schedule a treasure hunt in Tracy's car.

But she had been smart enough to park in a prominent spot. Anyone coming or going from the church passed her old Ford, and it was clearly visible to anyone driving around the village green.

It was getting more and more difficult to pretend that he and Tracy were mere acquaintances. Tonight Sheila deliberately plunged a knife into Tracy's heart. Leaving Tracy alone in the bell room was the hardest thing he'd done all day. When he saw that wounded look in her eyes, he wanted to take her in his arms and kiss away the hurt.

It had been a serious mistake to kiss her on her birthday. He relived that moment too many times, waiting for a chance to hold her in his arms again.

But he needed to keep up the act. No one would believe in her innocence if they thought he was personally involved with her. Diaz already hinted that he was too soft on Tracy. And too many people were quick to swallow the rumors about her. They would immediately assume the worst—that she played up to him so that he would cover up for her crimes.

As though it wasn't enough for Tracy to be implicated in the theft of Ronda Starr's jewelry, Sheila heaped more coals on her head. Apparently Sheila would do anything and everything to drive Tracy out of the church, or better yet, out of Allerton.

He spotted Tracy coming out of the building. Her face was tense with worry as she surveyed the parking lot. When she caught sight of his SUV, she gave him a hesitant wave. He knew his strange behavior had her confused. He returned a salute and then waited until she drove out onto the street.

He turned to the boys in the back seat. "OK, guys, buckle up. We're off." He followed Tracy out of the parking lot. What he really wanted to do was to follow her all the way home, but he fought the temptation.

He forced his attention back to Mark and Luke. "How did your choir rehearsal go tonight?"

"I got to sing a solo," Luke announced proudly.

"All right!" Leif cheered. "A star is born."

"Uncle Leif," Mark called, "did Miss Dunn say her ring was lost?"

Leif swallowed a groan. "Yes, she misplaced it. We all looked for it, but no luck."

Mark hesitated. "I think I saw her put it in her musicfolder."

Leif slammed on the brakes. "You what?"

"When Luke and me were looking in the door, she was taking off her gloves. I could tell by the way she twisted and pulled on her finger that she was taking a ring off too inside her glove. And then she put the gloves in her folder."

Mark wouldn't deliberately lie, but he could be

mistaken. "Are you sure of that, Mark? You're not just saying that because you like Miss Dixon?"

"No, sir," Mark insisted. "I watched Miss Dunn because she was acting so funny."

Leif swung a fast U-turn and raced back toward the church. If Rev. Jim was still there, the doors would be unlocked.

The tires squealed as he brought the SUV to a halt by the back door. The pastor's car was still in the parking lot. "Boys, don't move. I'll be right back."

Leif dived out of the car. He almost broke into a run as he raced through the door and down the hall to the handbell room. The ringers' folders were all neatly arranged in order on the shelf. Tracy had put a label on the inside cover of each folder with the ringer's name. Fumbling in his haste, Leif finally located Sheila's folder.

Each folder contained a plastic pocket where the ringers stored their gloves and their pencils. Carefully Leif groped inside the pocket. As his fingers closed around Sheila's gloves, he felt the hard lump inside. He pulled the gloves out and shook the contents onto the bell table. There it was—Sheila's opal, glowing with iridescence.

Furious, he snatched up the ring and shoved it in his pocket. If Allerton were old Salem, the townspeople would have burned Tracy at the stake by now. He should report the incident to the pastor, but first he was going to set things right.

The boys were fidgeting by the time he returned to the SUV. "Uncle Leif, hurry up," Mark pleaded. "We won't have any time to play before bedtime."

Leif would move the world for his nephews, but tonight they would have to wait. "Sorry, guys, but we have to make one more stop before we go home. I'll ask your Mom to let you stay up an extra half hour tonight."

"Did you find the ring?" Luke piped up.

"I found it. I want to return it to Miss Dunn

tonight. Mark, I'm glad you saw what happened, but why didn't you say something when we were looking for it?"

Mark hesitated. "Miss Dunn—Miss Dunn doesn't like me. I was afraid she would say I was lying, and nobody would believe me."

Mark was probably right. "That's OK, pal. Buckle up again. This won't take long."

Sheila lived with her parents in a comfortable old farmhouse about a mile from the church. Leif suppressed the impulse to hammer the door down. He knocked politely,

Sheila answered his knock. She gave him a radiant smile. "Leif, what a nice surprise. Come in."

"Not right now." He gritted his teeth. "The boys are in the car. I just came to return your stolen property." He reached for her hand and slapped the ring into her palm.

The smile vanished as the color drained from her face. "How—where—where did you find it?"

"You know where," he snapped.

"Well, I—I ..." She looked down at the ring, avoiding his eyes.

"You owe Tracy an apology. You are going to call her tonight. Not tomorrow. Right now."

"Yes, Leif," she whispered.

Leaving her shaken, in the open door, he turned his back and stamped down the stairs to the SUV.

****

The days were growing longer, and it was not quite dark when Tracy reached home after handbell practice. Time to take Thor outside. Maybe a little fresh air would blow away her gloom.

Thor loved the back yard. He always started by racing to the stone wall at the back of the property with his big feet flopping, and then trotting back to sit at her feet with his tongue lolling happily. And then he chased anything that moved—butterflies, insects, dragonflies. He even looked wistfully up at the birds.

Sometimes she threw a ball for Thor to chase, but instead of retrieving it, he would parade around the yard holding the ball in his mouth. He didn't grasp the concept of the word "fetch."

By the time darkness fell and she led the puppy inside, she felt a little more cheerful. No matter what Sheila Dunn thought, she had a lot of allies. She hoped Leif was still in her camp although no one could tell that from his icy attitude.

The ringing of the phone interrupted her thoughts. She glared at the phone, debating whether or not to pick up the receiver. She was in no mood for conversation. Several times in the past week, she had answered the phone to hear nothing but a fast click and then a dial tone.

If this is another of those hang-up calls, I'm going to scream. It might be some absent-minded caller who kept dialing the wrong number. Or maybe it was one of Keith Bradford's fans—some "good citizen" trying to drive her out of Allerton.

Or what if it was someone trying to find out if she was at home? Ordinarily she would still be at church at this hour on a Wednesday evening. Could it be Rick Timmons? That thought sent a blip of alarm across her radar screen. She could be in danger if Rick was getting desperate.

She needed to get caller I.D. Of course, Rick would be smart enough to make his calls from a pay phone. A better idea would be to replace Jeff's broken answering machine. The machine would screen the calls, or if nothing else, it would cut off the endless ringing.

The phone continued to ring. Someone was very persistent. It has to be Mom returning my call, she decided. She forced herself to pick up the receiver.

"Hi, Mom," she said, trying to inject a note of cheer into her voice.

"Tracy, this is Sheila Dunn."

Not again. Tracy braced herself for another tirade about her dishonesty. "Yes, Sheila," she said coolly, waiting to hear the newest accusations.

"Tracy, I owe you an apology."

"A what?" She must be hallucinating. Did Sheila really say the word "apology?"

"Leif found my ring." Sheila hiccupped as though she had been crying.

"Leif?" Tracy began to doubt her hearing. "Where—where was it?"

"It was still inside my glove in my folder."

"Oh, I'm so glad to hear that." *No one could imagine how glad.* "It's such a beautiful opal."

"Yes, I'm very relieved. I thought you would want to know right away." There was a decided quaver in Sheila's voice.

"Thank you so much for calling." Tracy was ready to celebrate with a victory parade around the living room.

"I'll see you later." Sheila ended the call abruptly.

"Thor." Tracy flung her arms around the puppy. "Can you believe it? Leif came to the rescue again."

Thor wagged his whole body in delight. He seemed very pleased by her announcement. She hummed the chorus of "Thank You, Lord" while she found a special treat for the puppy.

By the time she called her mother, cleaned up the kitchen, and watched the evening news, Tracy was ready for bed. The ups and downs of this evening's emotional roller coaster had left her limp. Thor eyed her bed, but she conned him into his own spot in the corner of her room. He trampled his blanket and settled down, cuddling up to his rag doll.

She usually lulled herself to sleep by reading until her eyes closed. But no reading tonight. She was too tired to pick up a book. She turned off the lamp on her nightstand and then lay there wide awake, staring into the darkness.

She found herself mulling over Sheila's story. Something didn't add up. How on earth did Leif find the opal ring? He was already sitting in his SUV when Tracy left the building. And she thought Sheila had checked her gloves. Oh, well, Sheila had her ring back and more importantly, Leif knew she was innocent. That was what mattered. She closed her eyes and gave in to her weariness.

A ferocious racket blasted her out of a sound sleep. She sat bolt upright, staring into the darkness. She could barely see Thor at the dormer window, his paws on the window seat, barking ferociously. He sounded like a whole pack of hounds.

With trembling hands, she turned on the table lamp. Either the house was on fire or Timmons had come to reclaim the jewelry. She tiptoed to the window and peered out into the night.

The glow of the streetlight was dimmed by the giant oak tree. It gave just a faint bit of illumination to the front yard. She made out a shadowy figure moving quickly away from her car. Over the pounding of her heart and the din of Thor's barking came the roar of an engine and then the screech of tires as a car sped away.

Tracy's breath came in short, fast gasps. She sat down heavily on the floor and forced herself to take a long, deep breath. *Thank you, Lord.*

Thor nudged her with a cold wet nose. Still shaking, she ruffled his fur. "Good dog," she whispered.

She sat there unmoving, staring at the clock. Two in the morning. No point in calling Leif now. It was too late for him to do anything tonight. Timmons was at least five miles away by now. But Leif had told her to call anytime, day or night. He would give her an earful if she didn't let him know about the incident.

She mustered the strength to move to the edge

of her bed and grope for the phone. She punched in Leif's number with unsteady fingers.

He answered on the first ring. "Chief Ericson." He sounded as alert as if he had been waiting for her call.

"Leif," she managed, "it's Tracy. Thor woke me up. Someone was here—in the driveway—by my car. He's gone now."

"Are you all right?" Alarms rang in Leif's voice.

"I'm a little shaky," she admitted.

Assured she wasn't hurt, Leif assumed cop mode again. "Were you able to identify the person? Was it Timmons?"

"I'm sorry, Leif. It was too dark. All I could see was a shape running away and then a car taking off."

"Can you identify the car—the make, the style?" He rattled off questions faster than a quiz show host.

"No, he didn't turn on his headlights." Calmer now Tracy tried to recreate the picture of that car speeding away. "It was a dark color, but that's about all I could see."

"Which way did he go?"

"Away from town, toward Plymouth." At least she could tell him something. "He was really burning rubber."

Leif hesitated. "Do you think he had time to get into your car?"

"I don't think so. Thor really earned his keep tonight."

"OK. I'm coming by to check the tapes and see if that back seat has been moved. Don't go outside."

"No chance of that." Tracy doubted she would have the nerve to go outside for a week.

"Right now I want you to program your cell phone with my number on speed dial. If anyone so much as looks cross-eyed at your car, I want you to push that button."

Tracy gave him a shaky laugh.

"Now, go back to bed and get some rest." He paused. "Sleep tight."

"Right," she groaned. There was as much chance of her sleeping tonight as there was of Sheila Dunn sending her a bouquet of roses.

Thor wanted to join her in bed, and she was tempted to let him, but she managed to coax him back into his corner. She crawled wearily under the covers. She was still staring at the ceiling when morning came.

****

Tracy loaded her groceries into the back seat of her car. Just looking at that back seat cushion gave her a creepy feeling. Leif found the tapes were still in place. Apparently Timmons did not have time to discover that his loot was gone.

Pulling out of the store parking lot, she glanced at her watch. Ouch. She was running out of time. Grocery shopping took longer than she expected. So much to do, but she was due at work in an hour. She would have to settle for putting away the food that needed refrigeration and leave the rest of her load for later. But Thor would need a visit to the backyard and she had to change into her uniform.

She groaned aloud as she approached her house. Keith's Maserati sat in her driveway again. What did the man want now? Why wasn't he in Boston making speeches or passing laws or whatever state representatives were supposed to do?

She parked her car in the swale in front of the house. She didn't want to park behind Keith and block his exit. He was already getting out of his car with that phony smile on his face.

Snatching up the bag of frozen foods, she hurried up the driveway. "Keith," she said coolly, "I'm sorry. I don't have time for a visit right now. I'm late for work."

"But we need to talk," he protested. "I'll just come in for a minute."

"No, you can't come in. I'm in a hurry."

Keith's frown revealed his irritation. She should know that common folks just didn't say no to Mr. Distinguished State Representative Bradford. "I have some important information for you."

"Then tell me now or call me tomorrow." She would not relent.

Keith hesitated, but finally seemed to get the message. She was not going to let him in the door. "Well, the good news is that I received the check from the insurance company for Jeff's car."

"That's good." She wondered why that news required a personal visit.

"They gave him book value plus a little extra for the special fittings. I'm sure the car was worth more than that, but you know how these insurance companies operate."

"Yes, I do." Tracy shifted the grocery bag to the other arm.

"I'll deposit the check in Jeff's account tomorrow."

"That will be fine." She tapped her foot impatiently.

"Now the bad news, Judge Whitby recommended that the court deny your petition to be named conservator of Jeff's assets."

Tracy tried not to let Keith see her disappointment. "I expected that."

"There's a possibility that I'll be appointed conservator, so we can continue to work together." He gave her his trademark sly wink.

The thought of seeing more of Keith was enough to make her ill, but she swallowed the sour taste in her mouth. "I understand." She gritted her teeth. "Is that all? I really have to go."

"Well, there's one more item that might be of interest to you." Keith seemed to be licking his chops over this last tidbit.

"And what is that?"

"Before the court appointed Judge Whitby as guardian ad litem, your dear friend the police chief was offered the job. He turned it down."

That hurt. Tracy felt the pain like a knife in the heart. If Leif really believed in her, why would he refuse the chance to help her? She forced herself to keep a poker face, trying to ignore Keith's triumphant smile.

"Thank you for the information." She lifted her chin. "I'll see you in church." Turning her back so that Keith couldn't see her tears, she marched briskly to the front door.

CHAPTER XIV

Thor leaned contentedly against the old plaid sofa as Maggie scratched his neck. He was a sucker for anyone who found that magic spot under his collar.

"Maggie, I was such an idiot." Tracy bit back tears. Some hurts were too deep for pain. She felt hollow inside – an emptiness at the core of her being. "I vowed I would never give another man the power to hurt me. And then I fell for Leif."

"You're not an idiot," Maggie broke in.

"You think not? I was actually dumb enough to believe he felt something special for me. And he seemed so different from other men—a real Christian, honest and straightforward. But he's just like the rest of the male species. When you think you can count on them, they bail out."

"Tracy, you're not stupid, you're blind," Maggie insisted. "Leif is crazy about you. Haven't you seen that look in his eyes when he sees you, like he's melting inside?"

Melting? That was a laugh. All Tracy saw in his eyes was suspicion. "If he's so crazy about me, why didn't he accept the appointment as guardian ad litem. How can he say he believes in me and then turn down a chance to help me?"

"I'm sure he had a good reason." Maggie always played attorney for the defense.

But Tracy shook her head. "I should have known

from the start that it was all an act. He was always around, playing Good Samaritan—driving me to the hospital, driving me to church, driving me to work. And little dum-dum me—I was flattered by all the attention. But he was just being a cop, keeping an eye on a dangerous criminal who might corrupt his precious town."

"Maybe you were just a suspect at first," Maggie reasoned, "but don't you see? When he got to know you, he found the real Tracy behind all the rumors."

"So, he let them sic Judge Whitby on me."

"Tracy, use your head. Leif must have turned down the appointment weeks ago, before he really knew you."

"Well, all I know, is I'll be glad when Rick Timmons is behind bars and Mr. Police Chief isn't hovering over me every minute. If it weren't for Jeff, I'd go back to New York and forget I ever heard of Allerton."

"You don't mean that," Maggie protested.

Tracy hesitated. No, she didn't mean it. Three years ago she had run away from Allerton, too much of a coward to face a man's betrayal. But she would never run again. Allerton was home. No matter what Leif did or said, her church family had rallied around her. She didn't want to leave Maggie again, and she wouldn't abandon Rev. Jim and her bell ringers.

Maggie frowned as she glanced at her wristwatch. "Tracy, I don't like leaving you like this, but I have to go. We've got a new boarder arriving this afternoon. But, I'm going to tell you one last thing. Leif Ericson is in love with you."

"Sure he is." Tracy made a face. "But thanks for letting me unload on you."

"That's why God invented friends." Maggie gave her a hug at the door.

Tracy fought back tears as her best friend drove off. So Maggie thought Leif was in love with her. *As if.* She knew one thing for sure—she was in love with Leif—head over heels, and there was nothing she could do about it.

But she wouldn't give in. She closed the door and straightened her shoulders. No more weeping and moping. Broken heart or no, she would concentrate on something else. She needed to mark the colors on the new handbell music.

Some of her ringers were learning to actually read the notes, but a few of them still looked for those red and blue circles. She dreaded their next rehearsal. Could she bury her feelings while she looked at Leif's stony face?

Her gloom was shattered by the ringing of the phone. She was in no mood to talk right now, but she hadn't found time to hook up the new answering machine. It was still sitting in the box. She should probably tell Leif about the hang-up calls, but she had no intention of telling Leif anything, ever again.

But the phone went on ringing. If she was lucky, it would be another hang-up. She picked up the receiver. "Tracy Dixon," she said listlessly.

"Miss Dixon, this is Dr. Burrows."

Tracy's heart stopped. "Dr. Burrows! What's happened? Is Jeff—is Jeff ..." She trailed off, unable to make herself say the words.

"I really should wait until I could tell you this in person, but I felt you should know immediately." The doctor hesitated. "The man we are treating here is not your brother."

Stunned, Tracy sat down hard. "What—what did you say?"

"The man you have been visiting here is not Jeffrey Dixon."

Tracy's breath became ragged. "But—but—that can't be possible. Who is he? Where is Jeff?"

The doctor sounded weary. "I'm sorry, but I don't know the answers. We're trying to identify our patient, but we have no way of knowing where your brother is."

"How—how do you know this? How did this happen?" Her mind wouldn't accept his words.

"When the patient arrived here, we were told that he was Jeffrey Dixon. We were only concerned with saving his life. When we got him through the resuscitation stage, we sent for his medical records from the VA hospital. That's when we noticed that some things didn't fit. The blood type was the same, the age was about right, but the records showed that Jeffrey Dixon had lost his right leg from the knee down. Our patient was missing only his right foot."

The doctor heaved a deep sigh. "We checked with the state police who were at the scene of the accident. They said the victim's wallet and identification were totally destroyed, but the car was registered to Jeffrey Dixon. That didn't resolve our problem, so we managed to obtain Jeffrey's dental records. They clearly did not match our patient. I don't know what else I can tell you except that this man is not your brother."

All Tracy managed was a feeble "Thank you." She sat motionless in a state of shock. *Not her brother? Then who was he? And where in the world was Jeff?* Maybe he had been thrown out of the car. He could be lying in a ditch somewhere where nobody had found his body. She stared at the telephone. She didn't want any further contact with Leif, but there was no one else who could help her.

Her hands were trembling so violently she barely pressed the numbers on the phone. In spite of all her resolves, she felt a wave of relief when she heard that deep voice. "Chief Ericson here."

"Leif," she breathed, "It's Tracy. I just got a call from Dr. Burrows. The man in the burn center—the man we've been visiting—it's not Jeff."

Total silence.

Tracy panicked. Had he hung up on her? "Leif, are you there? Did you hear me? Jeff could be lying in a ditch somewhere,"

"I heard you, Tracy. Are they sure?" Leif sounded as stunned as she was.

"The man's injuries are different and the dental records don't match. The doctor is positive it's not Jeff."

"Then Jeff may be alive and well." Leif's voice was jubilant.

"We don't know that." Tracy fought back a sob. "If he's alive, where is he?"

She felt Leif's excitement. "I think I know. Sit tight for a few minutes while I make a phone call. I'll call you right back."

Tracy sat frozen in her chair, torn between joy and despair. This was all so bizarre. It had to be a dream. She would wake up and find that she had just imagined that call from Dr. Burrows.

Thor nudged her knee, demanding attention. Apparently she was awake. She stooped to stroke the puppy's head. "Thor, there's a chance that—maybe—Jeff is OK."

It seemed like an eternity until the phone rang again. She snatched up the receiver. "Tracy," Leif was almost shouting. "All is well. I'm on my way. I'll be at your house in one minute."

She stood staring at the receiver in disbelief. *All is well. All is well?*

When Leif pulled his SUV into the driveway, she was already running out the door to meet him. Grinning broadly, he stepped out of the car and swept her into his arms. Crushing her against his broad chest with her feet dangling a foot above the ground, the staid, stoic chief of police danced her in circles around the front lawn.

Caught up in his exhilaration, Tracy clung to his broad shoulders. Her head spun as though she were riding the Octopus at the Brockton Fair. She was dizzy and breathless when he set her on her feet again, but he smothered her with a hug and a kiss that sent her senses reeling.

"Oh, Leif," she gasped when she came up for air. "Jeff is alive? You know where he is?"

Leif seized her hand and tugged her toward the house. "Come inside and I'll tell you the whole story."

****

Leif put his arm around Tracy as they settled on the sofa. He liked the way the sagging cushions forced her to snuggle against his side. He heaved a sigh of contentment. "I guess I need to start at the beginning. Do you remember that I told you Jeff and I became good friends and he started going to church with me?"

He felt Tracy's nod against his chest.

"Jeff tried to cut back on his drinking, but he didn't seem to have the will power to stop. He'd go several days without a drink and then go off on a binge again." Leif remembered his disappointment every time Jeff fell off the wagon.

"Rev. Jim and I decided to try an intervention. We dropped in on Jeff one Sunday after church and laid it on the line. Jeff didn't take it well. He was angry and defiant at first, but he finally admitted he needed help. We prayed with him to accept help from the Lord." Leif paused. He decided not to tell Tracy that her big, strong brother had broken down in tears.

"There's an alcoholic rehabilitation center at that Christian retreat up in Chilton. Even before we confronted Jeff, Rev. Jim made arrangements to enroll him in their three-month program. When Jeff finally admitted that he needed help, we got him packed and on his way before he could change his mind. Jeff drove his own car and Jim rode along with him to be sure he got there. I followed in my car so Jim rode back with me. We stayed long enough to make sure Jeff was admitted. That was the last time I saw him."

"But where is he now?" Tracy sounded bewildered.

Leif pulled her closer. "He's still there. Safe and sound."

"Safe and sound! Why didn't you tell me about this?"

He had debated telling Tracy the whole story right from the start. Perhaps he had made the wrong decision. "Tracy, I'm sorry. I left Jeff at the center one day and then heard about the accident the next. I assumed he quit the program right off the bat without giving it a chance and he was headed for home when he went off the road. I guess I should have told you that first day when we visited the hospital, but you were so distraught over his condition."

Tracy looked dazed. *Could he make her understand?* "I talked it over with Rev. Jim. We felt it wasn't the right time to tell you—that it would only make you feel worse to know that he ran away from rehab. We decided to wait until Jeff's condition improved. We weren't trying to hide anything from you."

Tracy was silent. Maybe he had been too abrupt. Was she angry that he had waited so long to tell her Jeff's story? But she finally spoke in a breathy whisper. "If Jeff is all right, why hasn't he called to let me know where he is?"

Leif was relieved. She sounded more confused than angry. "The patients aren't allowed any outside contact for the first six weeks. No phone calls, no visitors. It's all part of the program."

"But who is the man in the burn center?"

The $25,000 question, and Leif didn't have the answer. "I guess Jeff knows who was driving his car, unless the guy stole it."

"When can we see him?" Tracy began to sound excited as though the news was finally sinking in.

"His six weeks aren't up yet, but I got special

permission for us to visit with him today. They'll let us have a half hour." It had taken Leif some fast talking to convince the director that he wasn't making up the strange story.

"Today!" Tracy's eyes lighted like a child's on Christmas morning.

Her smile always turned him to mush. "We can go whenever you're ready."

"I am so ready." She bounced to her feet. "Just let me put Thor in the kitchen."

Watching her hurry away, Leif felt a flood of joy. He had just blown all his plans to act distant and indifferent. He blew them and it didn't bother him a bit. He had been waiting a lifetime to find the girl of his dreams. Was this the woman God had chosen for him?

****

Tracy perched on the edge of her chair in the visitors' room, waiting for her brother to appear. If she were a nail-biter, she would have chewed her way down to her elbows by now. Sitting beside her, Leif pretended to be cool and calm, but he wasn't a very good actor. He was as excited as she was.

The building was made of logs in the style of the lodge at Yellowstone National Park. The wicker chairs in the large room were arranged in conversational groups. She and Leif were the only visitors, but Tracy realized they were granted a special privilege.

They had been waiting forever. She stared at her watch. Well, they had waited five minutes.

But suddenly the door opened and Jeff appeared. Tracy's jaw fell open. His shoulders were back, straight and proud. Instead of hunching over crutches, he used a cane. She could tell that he was wearing the prosthesis on his leg. She surged to her feet and rushed across the room to throw herself into his arms.

Jeff hugged her close and then took a step back

to stare at her in confusion. "Tracy, it's really you. What are you doing here? And Leif, too?" His smile was pure sunshine.

"It's a long story, pal. We have a few mysteries to solve." Leif grasped Jeff's hand and the two men exchanged a long look.

"Jeff, you look wonderful." Tracy clung to his arm. This was the brother she knew. His deep blue eyes were clear and sparkling and his dark hair neatly trimmed. The last time she saw him, Jeff's eyes were glazed and unfocused and his hair was a shaggy tangle.

Jeff planted a kiss on her cheek before they sat down together in front of the big fieldstone fireplace. "You look good to me, too, Sis, but what's going on? I wasn't supposed to have visitors until next week."

Leif took the lead. "We need to start with a question. Do you know what happened to your car?"

Jeff looked puzzled. "Sure, I loaned it to a friend, an old army buddy. I figured it would just be sitting in the parking lot for three months, and he needed wheels. Is something wrong?"

"Jeff, your friend was in an accident." Leif broke the news gently. "He's in the burn center at Mass. General. Your car was totaled."

"Ron Carter?" Jeff stiffened as though he had suffered a heavy blow. "Is he all right?"

Tracy fought back tears. She had to add to Jeff's pain. "Your friend was horribly burned. All this time we thought it was you lying there. We went in to the hospital every week, just praying that you would make it."

"Every week! When did this happen?"

"Monday, the day after we checked you in here," Leif explained. "When I heard about the accident, I figured you had given up and left the program."

Jeff gave them a sad smile. "No, you and Rev. Jim are powerful prayers. You prayed me in here to stay."

Leif frowned. "I'm surprised no one here saw the article about the accident in the newspaper."

"I remember now," Jeff said. "Someone told me about the article, but the newspaper spelled the name Dickson. The guys were kidding me about the similarities in the name, but nobody made the connection."

"Your friend's identification was burned, along with his clothes. The state police assumed you were the driver."

"But, why didn't Ron tell them?" Jeff looked thoroughly baffled.

Tracy took up the story. "They're keeping him in a drug-induced coma until the burns heal. They are so painful."

Jeff's face was lined with worry. "Is Ron going to live through this?"

Tracy forced a cheerful note. "The doctor is very encouraged. The skin grafts are adhering."

"But he's going to be hospitalized for a long, long time," Leif added.

"Poor Ron." Jeff shook his head sadly. "He's the original hard luck kid. When I came back from Iraq, we shared a room at Walter Reid. Don't you remember him, Tracy?"

Tracy nodded, picturing Jeff's hospital roommate. He always looked so sad.

Jeff continued with his story. "Ron lost a foot and I was missing half my leg, so we did a lot of commiserating. We got to be really close friends, but after he was discharged from the hospital, we lost touch."

Tracy saw that Jeff was close to tears.

"I was surprised to run into him when I checked in here. He was living on the streets when the court ordered him into the program. The day I arrived here, he had done his time and was being released. But he had nowhere to go but back on the streets. No home, no job, no nothing. I gave him the keys to my car and the names of some people who might be able to help him get off the ground. And then this happened."

Tracy clasped Jeff's hand. "I know I'm being selfish, but I'm so glad it wasn't you under all those bandages. We'll keep praying for Ron, and we'll find a way to help him when he gets out of the hospital."

"We'll have to let the doctors know who he is," Leif put in. "They're still trying to learn his identity."

"Jeff, why didn't you tell me you were going into the program? If it weren't for Leif, I wouldn't have known where to find you." Tracy tried not to sound upset that no one had let her know what was going on.

"I sent you an e-mail," Jeff insisted, "on that Sunday just before I left home. Didn't you get it?"

Tracy blushed. Sunday, she thought. That was the day she had spent in the charming company of NYPD Detective Diaz, but she didn't want to worry Jeff with that information. E-mail had been the farthest thing from her mind that day. The message was probably still sitting in the in-box in her roommate's computer. Tracy hadn't read a message since then. "I guess I missed it."

"So, how's Mom doing? And Aunt Grace?" Jeff asked.

Tracy slapped a hand to her forehead to joggle her memory. "Oh, my goodness. I have to call Mom. She'll be thrilled out of her mind. She's been so worried about you, but she couldn't leave Aunt Grace. But Mom's doing well, and Aunt Grace is recovering from her surgery."

An officious woman in a business suit put her head in the door and pointed at the clock. Tracy didn't want to believe that their time was up already. She could sit and just stare at Jeff for hours, trying to convince herself this was all real.

"I guess we have to leave now," Leif said.

They were all reluctant to say goodbye. Leif shook Jeff's hand again and gave him a long brotherly hug.

Tracy stood on tiptoe to kiss Jeff's cheek. "I'm so proud of you, big brother," she whispered. "I can't wait until you're home again."

Jeff smiled broadly. "I'm proud of me too. I'm thinking of joining the human race again."

As Leif took Tracy's hand, Jeff raised a questioning eyebrow. "Hey, is there something going on with you two?"

Tracy felt a flutter of joy when Leif winked at Jeff and waved goodbye with crossed fingers. She tried to remember why she was never going to speak to Leif again.

CHAPTER XV

Leif eased off on the accelerator as he passed Tracy's house. Her car was not in the driveway. He groaned. Worry nagged at him whenever she was out of his sight. He prayed that wherever she was, there were crowds of people.

Normally he didn't drive patrol, but he was becoming more and more uneasy about Tracy's safety. It had been almost a week since Timmons tried to break into her car. Leif checked the tapes faithfully at least twice a day, but the back seat cushion had not been moved.

Timmons was bound to make another move soon. Years of detective work taught Leif patience, but this cat and mouse game played havoc with his nervous system.

And he was beginning to doubt his sanity. He must have been out of his mind to come up with this harebrained scheme to trap Timmons. The man was vicious. He needed to be locked away for eternity plus fifty years, but it wasn't worth putting Tracy's life on the line on the slim chance they could catch him in the act.

Why did she have to live at the far end of nowhere? How could he protect her twenty-four hours a day without making her a prisoner?

Marry her. The thought startled him so much he almost veered off the road. Marry Tracy! He really was out of his mind. But the more he thought about it, the more appealing the idea became. That lady had become a permanent fixture in his dreams.

There was just one big catch. How did Tracy feel about him? They had been through more than their quota of trauma over the past six weeks—supporting each other, crying together, laughing together. He held her in his arms in sorrow and in joy. And they shared a few much too brief kisses.

But Tracy had no faith in men. She had been betrayed by every man who was important to her, starting with her father when she was just a kid. And he let her down too—refusing to accept guardianship of Jeff, failing to tell her about Jeff's rehab program, pretending there was nothing special between them. He tried to explain his reasoning to Tracy, but did she believe him?

He would table the idea of marriage until he won her trust, but he wouldn't give up.

He sorted through the possible courses of action. It seemed that the only way to protect her now would be to make the news public that the jewelry had been found. When that hit the headlines, Timmons would give up the hunt and disappear. He would literally get away with murder, but Tracy would be safe.

Leif rolled into the parking lot behind the station and sat staring through the windshield, his brain churning. Announcing the find would create another problem. When the news came out that the jewelry had been recovered, Tracy would be in more trouble. Detective Diaz would be convinced that she was Timmons's accomplice—that Rick hadn't come back to look for the jewelry again because Tracy warned him away. Diaz wouldn't waste any time getting a warrant for her arrest.

Leif was snared in a Catch 22. With a choice between bad and worse, the important thing was what was best for Tracy.

Three more days, he decided. He'd give their

plan three more days. If Timmons didn't make a move, Leif would phone Diaz and tell him to release the news to the media. And then Leif would fight the whole New York Police Department to convince them that Tracy was innocent.

****

The Fisherman's Landing was busier than ever on a Friday night. The Landing was always a popular spot, not only for the fabulous seafood, but for the ambiance. The décor captured the lure of the ocean—fish nets and bobbins, starfish and conch shells, scrimshaw and antiques, and sailboats in bottles. There were even authentic relics of the old sailing ships, including a genuine figurehead.

All Tracy's tables were full and she was running a marathon trying to keep up with the orders. But the tips were good and her financial situation looked brighter with every order she served. And better still, tourist season hadn't even started.

She was grateful to have her car again, but it came with problems attached—number one, staying on constant alert for another visit from Rick Timmons, and number two, paying off the debt for repairs to the tune of $1800.

And there was something else, although she hated to admit it. She missed the time she and Leif spent alone in the confines of his SUV. Through all their ups and downs, they developed a bond that seemed to be growing into so much more. Of course, she still saw him at church and at choir rehearsals, but they were always surrounded by a crowd. Leif tried to explain why he needed to act distant and aloof. He was sure that Detective Diaz would be suspicious of Leif's faith in her if the detective thought they were more than friends.

But maybe that wasn't the real reason they saw so little of each other now. Leif was probably relieved to give up his part-time job as chauffeur. She had certainly taken up more than her share of his time. And yet, the day they visited Jeff at the rehab center, they had been closer than ever. She treasured the memory of being crushed in Leif's powerful arms as he whirled her around the front yard. But that was a special occasion. Maybe she was making too much of that one exhilarating day.

As the evening wore on, the crowd began to thin out and Tracy took a moment to catch her breath. She stood near the planter box where her guests were able to signal if they needed her. And then that eerie feeling came over her again. The goose bumps were back. Someone was watching her.

Walking slowly among her tables, she refilled water glasses and checked her customer's needs while she made a quick survey of the dining room. No one appeared to be blatantly staring at her. Diners tended to pay more attention to their food and their companions than their waitresses until they needed something.

She wanted to blame her uneasiness on an overactive imagination, but she remembered the old adage—maybe you're paranoid, but that doesn't mean they're not out to get you.

A tall, well-dressed man talking to the headwaiter caught her attention. As she looked in his direction, he gave her a furtive glance from the corner of his eye. She felt a flutter of fear. She didn't recognize the man—jet black hair, a closely trimmed dark beard and mustache that framed his mouth, horn-rimmed glasses. She forced herself to look away, continuing to check on her tables. But something about the man set off alarms in her head.

She couldn't come up with a good excuse to interrupt the maitre d's conversation, but if she paid a visit to the ladies room, she would pass closely behind them. Putting on an air of nonchalance, she moved casually in that direction, pretending to be unaware of the two men.

The headwaiter was speaking. "If you'll call

customer relations tomorrow afternoon, they'll be happy to help you make arrangements for your party, Mr. Johnson."

"Thank you," the man responded. "You've been very helpful."

Tracy almost skidded to a stop. She knew that voice. It haunted her nightmares since the night of the theft. He had completely altered his appearance, but she would recognize that voice anywhere. Rick Timmons.

She forced herself to keep walking toward the restroom, groping for the cell phone in her pocket. Ducking around the corner, she punched the speed dial and whispered a prayer. "Please be there, Leif."

"Chief Ericson." That reassuring voice.

"Leif," she spoke just above a whisper. "He's here. Rick Timmons is here in the restaurant. He's not at a table. He's just talking to the headwaiter. I don't think he knows that I recognized him. But why would he take a chance and come inside?"

"He's checking to be sure you're going to be tied up for a while. Hold tight. I'm on my way."

Tracy peered cautiously around the corner. "Oh, no. He's starting to leave."

"Don't cut off the phone," Leif cautioned. "Keep the line open."

"I'm going to watch and see what he does now."

"Don't let him see you!" Leif was almost shouting.

As Timmons strolled out the door, Tracy darted up to the maitre d'. "I'm sorry, Mr. LeBlanc. I have an emergency. I have to leave—right now."

Unlike most headwaiters, LeBlanc tried to accommodate the employees. He glanced quickly around the dining room. "It's slow now. I'll tell Trisha to cover your tables."

"Thanks so much," she gasped. "I'll be here on time tomorrow."

Her purse was in her car, but her keys were in

her pocket. Still clutching her phone, she opened the front door a crack and peered out into the parking area. The lot was well lighted, but she didn't detect any movement. A laughing couple appeared. She strained to see them, but no, the man was short and stubby. It wasn't Timmons. The twosome located their car and drove away.

Hello, Tracy, she berated herself. Her car wasn't in the front lot. She parked it in the employees' area around on the side. Treading as quietly as possible, crouching close to the evergreen shrubs that lined the front of the restaurant, she made her way to the corner of the building. Forgetting to breathe, she put her head out just far enough to see her old Ford.

The dome light inside the car was lighted. Timmons had managed to open a door. Quickly she drew back. "Leif," she whispered, "he's inside my car."

"Tracy, for the Lord's sake, be careful. I'll be there in three minutes."

Tracy heard the slam of a car door and then the sound of heavy footsteps coming toward her. She plunged into the shrubbery, huddling in the shadows, hoping the glare of the neon sign wouldn't reveal her hiding place.

Timmons stormed across the parking lot. He had to be furious to discover that the little leather case was missing. He climbed into a low-slung sports car and slammed the door with the force of an explosion. "Leif, he's driving away. I'm going to follow him."

"No, Tracy, stop. Don't try that. He'll recognize your car. He's already facing a murder charge. He's got nothing to lose if he attacks you."

"But I can't let him get away." She raced toward her car. "Leif, he's leaving—south on Route 28. Driving a black sports car—a Porsche."

"I'll try to intercept him before he gets to Wareham. You stay put. Do you hear me? Stay where you are."

Disregarding Leif's warnings, Tracy leaped into her old Ford. She revved the engine and roared out of the parking lot, pushing the car to the limit. She gradually caught up with the Porsche. *Don't get so close that he can see you.* She eased off on the accelerator, hanging back, keeping her focus on those distinctive taillights.

Another car pulled onto the highway ahead of her. Her pulse shifted into high gear. It would be trickier to tail Timmons with another vehicle between them, but the other car would serve as a screen. She would not let herself lose him. He was pushing the speed limit, but he wasn't careening wildly as though he were trying to make a getaway. He didn't know he was being followed.

And then the Porsche made a turn. "Leif, he's turning east at the Sunoco station."

"Tracy, I told you not to follow him. Break off. Break off."

"I can't," she pleaded. *Leif doesn't understand.* Her future hung on winning this battle.

The car that had squeezed between them turned off. If Rick looked in his rearview mirror, he couldn't miss seeing her now. She dropped back a little further. The Porsche made another turn.

"He's turned into a motel, The Clamdigger," she croaked.

"Don't stop," Leif shouted. "Keep driving past the motel. Go ahead to that ice cream stand about two hundred yards down the road. Wait for me inside. I'm almost there, but he's out of my jurisdiction. I'll have to call in the sheriff."

As Tracy drove past the motel, the lights on the Porsche went out. The flashing neon motel sign gave her a quick glimpse of Timmons climbing out of his car. Had he noticed her old Ford creeping by?

Approaching the ice cream stand, she felt a stab of fear. The store was already closed, the parking area dark and empty. No refuge inside.

Clenching the steering wheel, she pulled in close to the building and turned off the headlights. She didn't know what a heart attack felt like, but she suspected she was about to find out. Peering out into the darkness, she counted the minutes. "Hurry, Leif, hurry. Don't let him escape."

****

Leif prayed for all he was worth as he raced toward the motel. He should have stayed on the main road. It was impossible to get up any speed on the winding back-country roads. He had radioed the sheriff's office and deputies were on the way, but Tracy was in danger.

The little fool. What if that murderer knew she was tailing him? Stopping at that motel could be a ruse. Timmons might have backed right out again the minute she passed and turned back the way he came to make his escape. Or, much worse, he could be continuing down the road, hunting for Tracy's Ford.

His adrenaline pumped like accelerant on a fire. In his years as a police officer there were times he had feared for his own life. But that fear was nothing compared to the terror that raged through him now. Tracy was out there alone with no way to defend herself. He'd give his life for her in a heartbeat.

He felt his heart leap into his throat when he realized the ice cream stand was closed. There was no one in sight. His heart sank slowly into place again as he glimpsed Tracy's car in the shadows. He swerved into the parking lot and skidded to a stop.

Plunging out of the SUV, he raced toward her car. She opened the door and fell into his arms. He wrapped her in a bear hug, clutching her tightly against his heart. If he didn't ease off, he'd probably crack one of her ribs. But he couldn't let go. As long as he held onto her, he knew she was safe. "Tracy," he breathed, "you scared the life out of me."

But she didn't seem to be afraid for herself. "Aren't you going to arrest him?" she mumbled into his chest.

He groaned. "I can't, sweetheart. I'm out of my jurisdiction. The deputies will be here in a few minutes."

She tilted her head back to look up at him. "But what if he gets away?" Those gorgeous eyes pleaded with him to take action.

He couldn't help himself. The only way to stop her questions was to lower his head and seal her mouth with a kiss. He didn't lift his head again until two sheriff's patrol cars swept into the parking lot.

CHAPTER XVI

Leif recognized the four deputies who arrived on the scene. He had worked with them before. Quickly he laid out the situation for Sgt. McNeill, the officer in charge, and they organized their plan of attack.

"Tracy, come with me," he called. There was no way he would leave her alone in the darkened parking lot at the ice cream stand. Timmons could be somewhere along the road right now searching for her.

She jumped in beside him as the sheriff's cars began to move out onto the road. "You're going to have to stay in the SUV," he warned as they followed the patrol cars out of the parking lot. "If you hear shots, get down on the floor and stay there."

For once Tracy didn't give him an argument.

"Describe Timmons for me."

"He's tall, over six feet, black hair in a brush cut, a close-trimmed dark beard and mustache, horn-rimmed glasses," she reported. "He was wearing a dark business suit. I think he might be using the name Johnson."

He smiled. Tracy was observant. She sounded like a trained investigator. She leaned forward in her seat, peering through the windshield as though that would help to speed up the arrest. The three cars rolled quietly into the motel lot and parked to form a barrier around Timmons's Porsche. That sporty little car wasn't going anywhere tonight.

The three deputies stood on sentry duty while he and Sgt. McNeill trooped to the motel office. A pasty-faced clerk looked up with an insolent expression, chomping on a wad of gum as they approached his desk. His expression changed dramatically when McNeill flashed his badge.

"We're looking for a man named Timmons," the sergeant said brusquely. "He may be using an alias."

The clerk's Adam's apple bobbed as he swallowed his gum. "We don't have a Timmons registered," he squeaked.

"Try the name Johnson," Leif said, repeating Tracy's description of Timmons.

"Oh, yes." The clerk looked relieved. "That's Mr. Johnson. Room 26."

"We need the key," the sergeant snapped.

"Do—do you have a warrant?" Leif watched as the clerk seemed to have an internal debate—would he rather be in trouble with the motel manager or with these two tough-looking lawmen?

"Would you prefer that we broke down the door?" Leif asked politely.

The clerk fell over himself in his rush to accommodate them. "Room 26," he gasped, producing the key.

McNeill signaled two of the deputies to station themselves outside, one in front and the other in back of the building. Timmons was not going to escape through a window. The third, Deputy Cabrera, followed as Leif and McNeill climbed the steps to the second floor. Room 26 was at the far end of the building. They moved swiftly and silently along the outside balcony.

Guns in hand, Leif and Cabrera flattened themselves against the wall. Sgt. McNeill stood to one side to avoid a bullet as he hammered on the door. "Open up, Plymouth County Sheriff," he shouted.

Expecting resistance, Leif was surprised when

the door immediately opened. The horn-rimmed glasses were missing, but otherwise the man was just as Tracy described him. He greeted them with a wide smile. "So, what can I do for you, gentlemen?"

Leif followed McNeill into the room, on alert for any wrong moves, but Timmons stepped back, waving them in as though he were hosting a dinner party.

"Rick Timmons, you are under arrest charged with murder and grand theft."

Timmons never lost his smile as the sergeant began reciting his Miranda rights. He held out his hands to accommodate Deputy Cabrera in handcuffing him and frisking him for weapons. Apparently he was clean.

"I'm afraid you've made a mistake," he said pleasantly. "My name is Johnson. Frederick Johnson. I have identification."

Leif picked up the horn-rimmed glasses that were lying on the dresser. "That's an interesting prescription you have for your spectacles, Mr. Johnson. Clear glass."

Still smiling, the man ignored Leif's comments. "I'm a salesman for Rinker Products. The main office is closed at this hour, but I have my supervisor's home phone number if you'd like to call him. He can confirm my identity. Or maybe you'd rather speak to my attorney about a lawsuit for false imprisonment."

McNeill paused, giving his prisoner the once over. "Watch him, Cabrera," he ordered. "I need to speak to Chief Ericson."

Leif followed McNeill out onto the balcony. The sergeant scowled. "What do you say, Chief? Are you positive we've got the right guy? He's a mighty cool customer."

Leif didn't hesitate. "I'll get Tracy. She can make a positive I.D." He realized that all his doubts and mistrust of Tracy were long gone. He had complete confidence in her.

Ignoring a stab of pain in his bad knee, he raced down the stairs and opened the door of the SUV. Tracy was waiting, tense with expectation. "Was he there? Did you get him?"

"We've got him, but are you sure this is Timmons? The guy is claiming we've got the wrong person."

"It's Timmons," she said flatly.

He hated to involve her any further, but they needed her. "Would you be afraid to face him and confirm his identity?"

"I'd be honored." Tracy gave him an excited smile as she jumped to the ground. "It will be a pleasure."

Timmons didn't flick an eyelash when Tracy followed Leif into the room. In spite of his handcuffs, he was still acting as though he were enjoying a social call from friends.

"Hello, Rick." Tracy looked him squarely in the eye. "It was so very kind of you to involve me in your crimes."

"And who is this young lady?" said Timmons cheerfully. "Charming."

Tracy put her chin up. Leif knew that was her battle flag. "You're not fooling anyone, Rick. Leif, if you'll check the palm of his left hand, you'll find an L-shaped scar from an old injury. As I recall, a firecracker blew up in his hand."

For the first time, Timmons showed a crack in his polished façade. "You don't have jurisdiction here, Chief," he muttered.

"Right," Leif agreed. "I'm just a consultant on the case."

"I have all the jurisdiction you can handle," Sgt. McNeill growled. "You're still in Plymouth County."

The deputy had cuffed Timmons's hands behind his back. Leif stepped around him and turned his left hand palm out. Tracy knew what she was talking about. "That's some scar, Timmons," he commented. "I bet that firecracker hurt like blazes."

Timmons's jolly-good-fellow attitude deflated as the air fizzled out of his balloon. He didn't offer a word of protest as Sgt. McNeill and Deputy Cabrera marched him out the door.

Leif and Tracy stood leaning over the balcony railing, watching as McNeill squeezed his prisoner into the back seat of the patrol car.

With his hands on her shoulders, Leif turned her to face him. She was aglow with triumph. She had won the battle.

With the arrest of Timmons, she was no longer a suspected criminal. He was free to express his feelings. But were they all one-sided? Had she forgiven him for letting her down? He wasn't afraid to confront a six foot man armed with a knife, but this little bit of woman terrified him.

He was touched to see tears of joy in her eyes. He held his breath as she stood on tiptoe to put her arms around his neck. "Thanks for believing in me."

He pulled her closer. He had been waiting so long for this moment. "You're very welcome," he murmured.

What kind of a Romeo was he? He groped for some romantic words to whisper in her ear, but his tongue was tangled. He was so in love with this woman, he couldn't find the words to tell her. The only way to communicate his feelings was with a kiss—a long, slow, lingering kiss.

****

Tracy kept one eye on Leif's SUV in her rear view mirror. Her Viking was still watching over her, following her home to be sure she arrived safely. It was after two in the morning by the time they pulled into her driveway, but she didn't want to say goodbye—not tonight, not ever.

"I know it's late, Leif, but can you come in for a cup of coffee? I'm too wound up to sleep."

"Twist my arm a little," he teased. Her heart

lifted as he took her key and unlocked the door.

Thor was yelping from the kitchen. Tracy felt a rush of guilt. "Oh, poor Thor. He's been shut up alone all this time." She rushed to free him.

Thor bounced out to greet them with enthusiasm. Tracy hugged the puppy, murmuring apologies. She scratched his favorite spot under the collar as she looked up at Leif. "I'm afraid I'm going to find a few puddles."

"Do you want me to take him outside?"

"That would be great. His leash is by the back door. If you'll give him a quick visit to the back yard, I'll put the coffee on."

By the time Tracy had mopped up a few accidents, Leif was bringing Thor in through the back door. He stood leaning against the door jamb, simply watching her. In the silence they were like two strangers, suddenly struck dumb by the intimacy of the place and the hour.

She busied herself with the coffee maker. Was this the end? Would Leif lose interest in her now that she was no longer the bait to catch Rick Timmons?

Wordlessly they carried their coffee into the living room, but as they settled on the sofa, the spell was broken. Leif put his arm around her and Tracy let her head fall onto his shoulder. Her heart told her that was exactly where it belonged. She wanted to freeze this moment and save it forever.

Leif smiled down at her. "I wish I could see Detective Diaz's face when I call and tell him that his suspect solved the case for him."

Tracy had to laugh. It would be a treat to see Detective Diaz speechless, that gravelly voice totally silenced. "Be sure to give him my love."

"You know, I was worried there for a while," he confessed. "Timmons is such a smooth operator; he had me wondering if you had made a mistake."

She nodded. "Rick could sell snowshoes in the

Sahara. Now you know how he convinced me he had an invitation to Ronda Starr's reception. If there was a contest for con artists, he'd win the grand prize."

"Did you ever tell Diaz about that scar on his hand? He faxed me a description of Timmons, but it didn't mention the scar."

Tracy sighed. "Leif, I was so scared and upset when Detective Diaz questioned me, I couldn't think straight. He asked me if Rick had any tattoos or scars or distinguishing marks. I thought he meant something in plain sight, like on his face or his neck, that would be visible to anyone who saw him."

"Well, you nailed him. That's what matters."

"We nailed him," she reminded him. "We never would have caught him if you hadn't trusted me." She paused. "What if I had been wrong?" she asked hesitantly.

Leif cupped her chin in his hand and caressed her cheek with his thumb. "I still would have believed in you," he whispered. "A guy has to trust the girl he's going to marry."

****

The Ericson's dining room was crammed to capacity. Besides herself, Tracy counted five Ericsons, two Scalias, and Rev. Jim. Leif's sister-in-law was determined to throw an engagement party despite her injuries. Anne directed traffic, supervising the preparations like a drill sergeant from her wheelchair.

Tracy felt like royalty with everyone else waiting on her. The side dishes came from the deli, but Leif grilled steaks on the outside barbecue. The tempting aroma of sizzling beef and charcoal smoke wafted through the screen door. Maggie brought her world famous chocolate chip cake. While Mark and Luke were setting the table, Val was balancing on his crutches, stringing up streamers and wedding bells.

It didn't seem possible that Anne had managed

to put this party together without word leaking out to the press. She had sworn the guests to secrecy, and everyone, including the boys, kept their mouths sealed.

Ever since the New York newspapers announced to the world that Ronda Starr's jewelry had been recovered, Tracy and Leif became the flavor of the month. They were under siege by the media who were intrigued by the story of the capture of the notorious Rick Timmons. Every talk show wanted an appearance by the courageous young woman and her handsome cop. Every magazine and newspaper wanted an interview with the romantic couple.

They agreed to an appearance on the Christian TV network, but once was enough. They turned down a barrage of lucrative offers to tell their story. But the reporters were ingenious. When they couldn't squeeze a comment from Tracy or Leif, they interviewed everyone else in the area, from Sgt. McNeill to LeBlanc, the maitre d' at the Landing.

The highlight for Tracy was when Keith Bradford proclaimed her the town's favorite daughter, the heroine of the community.

She prayed that the furor would subside before their wedding. Somehow it had become the most anticipated event in Plymouth County since the marriage of Priscilla Mullins and John Alden. She didn't want their precious day turned into a media circus. Leif's men offered to stand guard at the church and turn away anyone who appeared without an invitation. That sounded a bit drastic, but it might be necessary.

There would probably be photographers hiding in the bushes on the village green, but that couldn't be helped. Tracy had learned not to flinch when a cameraman popped out from behind the produce at the grocery store. If the clamor continued, they might have to send out invitations by registered mail, delivered by CIA agents.

When the steaks were ready, all her favorite people joined hands around the table. Anne called on Rev. Jim to say grace.

The pastor beamed with pride as though he was personally responsible for the love match. "Dear Lord, this is such a happy occasion, we are all filled with your love. Bless Tracy and Leif, give them a long and happy life together, and bless this wonderful food and fellowship."

"Amen," they all chorused.

Under the table Leif reached for Tracy's hand. She looked into his eyes and forgot there was anyone else in the room. The cop had captured her heart, locked it up, and thrown away the key.

She smiled now, remembering how hard she had tried to avoid Leif when she first came back to Allerton. But God knew best. He kept putting Leif in her path until she finally realized that this was the perfect man for her—strong, brave, honorable, compassionate, dependable. She needed a thesaurus to find all the right adjectives to describe how wonderful her man was. She sent up a small prayer of gratitude. Thank you, Lord, for finding Leif for me.

Maggie brought her back to the present. "So, when's the big day? I've been waiting too many years to be Tracy's matron of honor."

Tracy laughed. "Sorry about that, but I've waited too many years to find Leif. And now we have to wait a little longer. Jeff has four more weeks in the rehab program. We can't have a wedding until my brother is here to walk me down the aisle."

"Maybe I can get him released early," Leif suggested with a hopeful gleam in his eye.

"No way," Tracy protested. "Remember what Jeff said—you and Rev. Jim prayed him in there to stay."

"Hey, can I call you Aunt Tracy?" Mark piped up.

"You'd better," she threatened, "or I'll give that baseball back to Manny Ramirez."

"Aunt Tracy," Luke echoed, testing the sound of the name.

She had no idea what or whether she had eaten. She was already filled to the brim with love. She put her hand to her throat to touch the sapphire pendant Leif gave her as an engagement present. She cherished the words he whispered as he fastened the clasp at her neck. "It's almost as pretty as your eyes."

The pendant would be the "something blue" for her wedding. Her mother and her aunt were bringing "something old", diamond and sapphire earrings that were a family heirloom. "Something borrowed" would be Maggie's gorgeous wedding veil, a cloud of frothy white tulle studded with seed pearls. And "something new" was the perfect wedding dress that Lucille's granddaughter was making for her.

When the last crumb of Maggie's cake had been devoured, Leif got to his feet. "I have an announcement."

"Hear, hear," Maggie cheered. "The great stone face speaks."

Tracy's gaze locked onto Leif's face. He put his hand on her shoulder and she felt the depth of his love in his gentle touch. My cup runneth over."

He gazed down at her with that smile that affected her like a stun gun. "You know, I tried my best to resist this woman. I'm not sure exactly when I fell in love with her. It might have been when she let Luke bleed all over her. Or maybe it was when she made a bell ringer out of a guy with two left hands. But I think it was that day her car threw a rod. She was standing there in the middle of Main Street looking like a beautiful Cinderella whose coach had just turned back into a pumpkin. All I can tell you is that when that detective called from New

York, he gave me the best assignment I ever had—
'Keep an eye on Tracy Dixon.' Now, I take my job
very seriously, so believe me when I say I'm going to
keep my eye on Tracy Ericson for the rest of my life."

Thank you for purchasing this Wild Rose Press publication. For other wonderful stories of romance, please visit our on-line bookstore at www.thewildrosepress.com.

For questions or more information contact us at info@thewildrosepress.com.

The Wild Rose Press
www.TheWildRosePress.com

Printed in the United States
146734LV00001B/6/P

9 781601 545671